RECALLED

ANGEL FORCE
VOLUME 1

Greg Hibbins
©2015

Recalled

© 2015 by Gregory Hibbins

ISBN 978-0-9932747-0-1

Published by Caracal Books
United Kingdom
www.caracalent.uk

This is a work of fiction. Names, characters, incidents and dialogues are products of the author's imagination and are not to be construed as real. Any resemblance to actual events or persons, living or dead, is entirely coincidental.

The internet addresses, email addresses, and phone numbers in this book are accurate at the time of publication.

Cover design by Dawn Doyle
Cover photography – Seascape ©iStock.com/floriana
Cover photography – Soldier ©iStock.com/nstanev
Photo used for illustrative purposes only

*This book is dedicated to
all our men and women in uniform worldwide
who daily put their lives on the line
in the fight against extremism.*

PROLOGUE

North Eastern Border, Rhodesia (Zimbabwe)
September, 1979

Darkness hung over the land like a blackout curtain waiting to be drawn. The silence was deafening. Not even the crickets were singing. And then, with the suddenness so characteristic of Africa, the sun started to peek over the horizon. The first rays of light revealed the beauty of the land; the expanding rays illuminated the scene on the plains below. In the strengthening light, the beautiful morning soon gave way to the horror of what really lay on the open plains below.

What appeared to be rocks on the ground were clearly seen to be the bodies of men – men scattered all around in the grotesque poses of death. The bodies of once proud men lay scattered, broken, their dreams and visions lost for ever. On the cool morning breeze, the odour of gunpowder and high explosives hung in the air; this together with the smell of blood and sweat brought a rancid stench to the air.

Across this shocking scene, the crackle of a radio burst forth, "13 Golf, 13 Golf, this is Cyclone 1, do you copy?"

One of the lumps behind a bush moved, and the answering call went out, "Cyclone 1, Cyclone 1, this is 13 Golf. Copy."

"Roger, 13 Golf, we are two minutes out from your position and will be overhead shortly."

On the early morning wind came the sound of the approaching helicopters; Fire Force was on the way. A man rose from behind a bush and tossed a smoke canister into the open space before him. Within seconds orange smoke was billowing out.

"13 Golf, Cyclone 1, I have your smoke visual. Coming in now."

Like great fat birds the helicopters began to descend and deploy their troops; soon the ground was filled with men running to take up defensive positions. A tall figure breaking away from them moved toward the soldier who had tossed the smoke.

The tall man, a major so his epaulettes proclaimed, broke the silence first, "Looks like you had a good night's hunting, Hulk."

The soldier – a man of average height and build – replied with a wry grin on his face, "Yes Sir, Major Hobbs; it was a right old punch up. We estimate about two hundred *terrs* came in to our ambush area; I blew all my claymores and mini claymores, then we traded shots for quite a while. Eventually, Stinker and I went out and mopped up with grenades and rifle fire."

Major Hobbs smiled. He knew that short, concise report did not tell the full story of the horror and brutality of the violent clash.

"Any casualties?" he asked.

"No, Sir, just a few scratches and bruises; our guys are all fine."

"Hulk," said the major, his voice heavy with regret, "the rumours are true; Ian Smith is going to sign an agreement, brokered by the British, that will see Rhodesia being handed over for free and fair elections."

The young soldier's face hardened, his eyes like ice. "You mean all we have fought for, all that good men have died for, will come to nought. Free and fair elections – what a joke! We all know that butcher, Mudabe, will kill and intimidate the people and wrestle for control; this country is doomed. That's it, Sir! I'm done! I resign my commission, effective from the end of September."

The young officer swung on his heel and walked away. Major Hobbs shook his head, knowing that many more of his elite special force men would react the same way when the news broke. His eyes followed the young soldier as he wearily walked away.

"Major Hobbs, Sir." The major swung round to see his Fire Force Sergeant Major.

"Yes, Sergeant Major," he replied.

"Kill count, Sir. 170 CT dead. No wounded, no casualties to our forces, Sir."

Major Hobbs shook his head in wonder, "All those enemy combatants dead, the handy work of only eight Special Force soldiers, and the best military brain I have ever seen." He let his eyes rest on Hulk and his weary men as they clambered aboard two Allouette helicopters; and as he silently bid them goodbye on their last field of battle, his eyes filled with tears – tears of sorrow and of pride for all the special men who made up this amazing unit, soon to be remembered only in the pages of history and the minds of men.

**Andre Rabie Barracks, Salisbury, Rhodesia
September 30th, 1979**

"Knock, Knock," came the sound on Major Hobbs door.

"Enter!" he shouted.

Looking up, he saw Hulk standing there with a handful of forms. "Clearance certificates Sir, just need your signature and then I'm done; as of midnight, I'm a free man."

Major Hobbs' eyes drifted over the man before him, weighing him up in his mind. About 5 ft.9, slim waist, broad shoulders, heavy chest. His gaze floated upwards towards the young man's face – a young face, only 21 in years, but the eyes looking out told their own story. Old eyes that had seen the horrors of five years of war, a boy soldier grown into a man under the harsh Rhodesian sun.

Major Hobbs' eyes focused again on the young soldier's chest; four medal ribbons sat under the brown parachute wings. To a knowing eye they shouted out a story: Grand Cross of Valour, Silver

Cross, Bronze Cross – the three highest awards for bravery; completed by the General Service Medal, the quartet were the most awards ever given to one man, a young captain just 21 years old.

"Before I sign that form, Captain, I want you to answer two questions: how did you get the nickname, The Hulk? And what next?"

A smile broke out on the young man's face, "During my national service with the RLI, after a contact with a big bunch of gooks, we withdrew to base; I went off to have a shower, and when I returned someone had written 'Hulk' on my combat webbing vest. My guys said I reminded them of the big green guy in a fight, totally mad!!! After that it just stuck."

Major Hobbs smiled; he had seen the young soldier in battle and believed it. "And the future?"

"I believe God wants me to go to South Africa; I don't know why, but I'm sure I will find out when I get there."

"Give me the forms, Hulk; let's get it done." With one flourish of his signature, the major brought down the curtain on one of the most remarkable careers of the Rhodesian bush war.

The young captain straightened, came to full attention and saluted, his hand brushing the brown beret with the famous and feared silver osprey, "It's been a privilege to serve with you, Sir."

"Same here, Captain; keep in touch."

CHAPTER ONE

Perranporth, Cornwall, United Kingdom
May 2012

Doff! Doff! Doff! Doff! The fifty-something man's head jerked up from the book he was reading, his alert mind immediately registering the nature of the sound – four shots, double-tapped, high power rifle, very close.

Dropping his book, he darted through to his bedroom and picked up his wife's face mirror, gently angling it out of the window. Its small lens revealed the picture of an Arab man, with a shemagh scarf around his head, rifle in his hand and two dead bodies at his feet. Old Mr and Mrs Johnson from Unit 2, both in their seventies, were the victims of this man's shots.

The man jerked the mirror back, reached for his mobile phone; the screen flashed back at him, no signal! Moving quickly but quietly through to the lounge he picked up the landline phone; no dialling tone greeted him. It was dead as well.

The situation crystallised in his mind; a terrorist attack was going down in Perranporth, and the terrorists had somehow managed to take out all the land and mobile communications.

He was right. A quick fly over the town would have revealed the smoking ruins of the once tall mobile towers and the phone exchange. It would have further shown all the roads into town blocked by jack-knifed lorries full of heavy concrete blocks; the town was effectively sealed off. Terrorist three-man stop groups manned every blockage with rockets and heavy machine guns.

The man darted back to the window; up came the mirror again. The terrorist was moving closer to his unit, walking close to the building and upstream of the river that passed just behind the units. His mind racing, he quickly came up with a plan. Using the mirror to observe what was happening below from his first-floor lounge, he picked up the heavy planter made of solid bronze and filled with his favourite bulbs.

As the terrorist drew near, the man lobbed an apple from the window to land on the other side of the river; the terrorist's head swung round to identify the noise. With his eyes diverted away from the unit, the man dropped the heavy planter from the window.

"Crack!" came the satisfying sound of a breaking neck as the planter landed on the scarfed head of the terrorist below. Bounding down the steps, with an agility that belied his age, he ran into his study and threw open the sliding glass door that led out onto the patio below – the patio on which the terrorist now lay dead, his head crushed and neck broken by the heavy planter.

Grabbing the dead man, he pulled him inside, followed soon after by the planter, dented, but still intact. Quickly drawing the heavy curtains, the man bent down over the dead body. Hands, not even trembling, stripped off the webbing and weapons that were on offer – an FEG pistol and an AKM-47 assault rifle – and stowed them in a backpack. A Dragonov Sniper rifle, a Motorola radio and five hand grenades completed the haul. Popping the radio ear piece into his ear, the man listened intently as the terrorist commander was giving orders to his men in the centre of town, half a mile away from the man's unit.

"Gather all the people – men, women and children; get them to the square. Usaf, get the camera and satellite feed set up; it must be ready to broadcast when we slaughter them like the pigs they are. Today, we strike fear into the hearts of the infidels and stream their slaughter across the world, bringing hope to the faithful and fear to the infidels; we start killing at 12:30pm. Quickly! Now move!"

The man glanced down at his watch. 11:20 am. 1 hour before the carnage would begin. A cold dread filled the man. The town was full of friends; his son and daughter-in-law and new grandson, just 6 months old, were all down town this morning, caught up in the nightmare that was unfolding.

Bounding back up the stairs, the man pulled a steel trunk from under his bed; throwing the lid open, he gazed at the contents inside. The battle vest with the words 'Hulk' written on brought back a barrage of memories, but reminiscing was not on his agenda; there were people to save. As his hand reached for a plastic waterproof bag, he sent up an urgent prayer, "Lord, help me to help those in need. It's been 20 years since I fired a shot in anger; please release the old skills and give me your protection and a steady hand. Help me to terminate this evil that has visited our town."

Grasping the plastic bag, he pulled it out and opened it. He quickly powered up the Iridium Satellite phone within. As he dialled in the 999 emergency number, he allowed himself a wry smile; his wife could never understand why he insisted on keeping a sat phone. "Wasted money," she'd called it. Well, today, maybe the cost would save the lives of their family and friends.

"999 emergency room, please state your emergency."

"This is Dr Stuart Flavell. I live in Perranporth, Cornwall, and we are under terrorist attack. They have cut off all communications; I'm calling on my sat phone."

"Thank You, Sir. We do have reports of 10 coastal towns in Cornwall suffering the sudden loss of communications."

Ten towns! Could it be possible that the terror attack was being staged against ten towns simultaneously? Stuart's blood ran cold at the thought of the carnage that could be unfolding across Cornwall.

"999, I have confirmation of two local people and one hostile dead; the hostiles plan to massacre the town people at 12:30 pm."

"Stuart, please stand by for our local incident commander."

"Hi, Stuart, my name is Ron; please give me more details."

"Ron, the details are sketchy, but Arab-looking terrorists have taken over Perranporth and plan to kill the people on live satellite TV. I'm an ex-special force operator; I've been able to kill one and arm myself from his kit. I heard their plans over his radio."

"Roger, Stuart. Are you an ex HMF operator?"

"Negative, Ron. Rhodesia."

"OK, Stuart, thanks." There was the briefest pause before Ron continued sombrely, "Stuart, the situation is bad; we have very few resources on the ground in the South West, and most of those are in The North taking part in War Games. We are sending a detail of Special Force operators to your location; however, they will only be on-site in 55 minutes."

"Ron, that's going to be too late! I've got family in town; I need to do something now. Assign me a call sign, and I will update you when I can; perhaps use my old call sign, 13 Golf. Over."

"Okay, Stuart, 13 Golf it is. We have your sat phone number, will wait for your update. Good luck!"

"Ron, I don't need luck; I need a miracle, and I know Who can provide that. 13 Golf out. It's thumping time."

Stuart punched the phone's red button just as the radio crackled to life, "Ishmael, Ishmael, report your status. Over."

So, now the dead terrorist had a name, Ishmael. Reaching into the box again, Stuart drew out a crumpled sheet of cellophane paper; holding it close to the radio, he pushed the receiver and started to crackle the paper, "Say again, you are breaking up," the radio crackled again. "Ishmael, you are breaking up; the line is full of crackling. Push the send button if all is okay."

Stuart pushed the send button twice, "Okay, Ishmael, report in again in 30 minutes. Out."

Stuart reached once again into the box and pulled out his camo gillie suit. He quickly stripped off his clothes, and pulled on his wetsuit, followed by his gillie suit; camo cream from the box followed. Soon, the transformation was complete – gone was the fifty-year old man; in his place stood a soldier of indeterminable age. Strapping on the battle vest and side arms taken from Ishmael, together with some other items from the box, Stuart was good to go. Strapping the AKM over his shoulder, he fitted the silencer that had been in the bag to the Dragonov Sniper rifle, checked its magazine and cocked it.

Down the stairs, one last check with the mirror to see if the coast was clear, and he was out the door. Grabbing his prized piece of driftwood from his garden display, he merged with the river that ran outside the door – the river that ran down to the sea by way of the town, the river that would be his transport to the centre of town.

CHAPTER TWO

The small but fast-flowing river, swollen by recent rains, carried the driftwood down towards the sea. Attached to the drift wood was what, to the naked eye, seemed to be a bunch of soggy rags or sea weed; the only give away that all was not what it seemed was the rifle barrel, wrapped in rags, that protruded forward from the drift wood.

"Man, this water is cold," said Stuart to himself; then he broke into a grin, "Hope one of the resident eels does not decide to take a bite out of me."

The brief moment of levity was replaced by laser-like focus as the town drew closer. Eyes sweeping, Stuart's gaze latched onto another scarf-swathed figure standing on the river bank, close to the boating pond at the edge of town. From 15 metres out the rifle coughed, and the terrorist tumbled forward into the water, just as the driftwood drew level. The bunch of rags, now detached from the wood, caught the body and dragged it to the side. In a matter of minutes the body was stripped of all munitions and anchored to a safety grid; the last thing Stuart wanted was the body floating into town to alert the hostiles.

Stuart quickly stripped himself out of his gillie suit and, retaining the battle vest and munitions, started to creep up the bank. A quick recon with the mirror revealed no hostiles around the boating lake.

Moving quickly up the bank and over the road, Stuart crouched at the low wall surrounding the boating lake. The mirror, back in play, revealed a hostile with his back to Stuart, looking towards the town centre. In an instinctive move, up swept the rifle, and another hostile slid to the ground. Stuart darted across the road opposite Lloyds Bank, collecting the hostile on the way. Once again the hostile was stripped of any useful munitions and then dumped into a recycling bin.

Stuart knew the town well; his best vantage point would be from the roof above the Hot Chilli Seed, the local spice shop. Every sense alert for movement or danger, he quickly made his way there.

Once on the roof, and with the help of the trusty mirror again, the full horror of the scene was revealed. About 80 people were gathered together in a bunch; among them Stuart saw his son, Tom, together with Tom's wife, Trish, and their baby son, Sam. Cold dread washed down his spine, followed by a silent prayer.

"Lord, You have brought me thus far; thank you. Please empower me to use these long-forgotten skills to save these people and my family. Cover them and me with Your blood, and may Your warrior angels contend for us today."

As those words left him, Stuart felt a great calm fall over him, followed by a warm rush of renewed energy.

Checking which way the wind was blowing – past the people, then over him – Stuart knew he could risk a call without the sounds floating back to the hostiles. Punching the recall button on his Sat phone, Stuart heard an immediate answer, "13 Golf, is that you?"

"Roger, Ron, it's me; here is the sit rep. Seven hostiles in the square – four of them watching the hostages and three, including one who seems to be the MMTC, setting up cameras and a satellite dish. Just five minutes before they will be doing a radio check on their men again; what's the situation on assets to assist? Over."

"Stuart, not good news. Assets are still 15 minutes out. They will come in from downwind and deploy as close to the target as possible. Over."

"Okay, Ron. I'm going to have to go this alone then; just tell your assets not to shoot the short tubby guy in a wetsuit, camo-creamed up and armed to the teeth. Once the hostiles don't get an answer from the three men I took out, they will start to investigate; so I have to act now."

"13 Golf, say again; confirm 3 men down?"

"Roger that, Ron. Three down, seven to go. Out."

As Stuart hung up the sat phone, he knew he needed help. His son, Tom, who was part of the crowd, was a crack shot – trained to shoot from 3 years old.

I have to alert him and get a weapon to him. As Stuart thought about this, he peeked over the low wall surrounding the roof. Tom was about 10 metres away at the edge of the crowd, looking as though he was about to do something, which – unarmed as he was – would be suicide. Stuart flashed the mirror, catching Tom in the eyes; Tom looked up and Stuart gave him their 'be ready' sign. Tom briefly nodded, while his immediate guard was distracted by a baby crying.

"Shut that baby up!" the guard screamed. Then, with a look of fanatical malice, he raised his weapon toward the baby girl. All eyes were drawn to him. At that moment Stuart rose up and threw an AKM to Tom, who caught it in a deft move. Then, almost in unison, they opened fire on the hostiles; the four guards closest to the captives dropped dead, blasted by a hail of fire from Stuart and Tom. Like well-oiled machines the father and son team swung their weapons on the three remaining hostiles and with lightening quick precision dropped them as well.

"Tom!" Stuart shouted. "Help is on the way, but we need to hold off the stop groups that are blocking the way into town until it arrives. The stop groups will have heard the fire and will be here in minutes. Get the people into the supermarket and lock the doors. Don't open until you hear my voice."

As he spoke, Stuart tossed some spare mags across to Tom. The pouch flew through the air to land at Tom's feet.

Some of the people had run in panic; others were too shocked to move, until Tom's loud voice broke through to them and got them running into the supermarket close by.

Stuart picked up the sat phone again, "Ron, do you copy?"

"Roger, 13 Golf. I copy."

"Roger, Ron. Seven further hostiles down, captives free and in a place of safety. My son, Tom, is watching over them; he is armed. Please advise your assets; he has the people in the supermarket behind locked doors. I'm about to have some hostile company; I can see nine more hostiles advancing on the centre of the town. I'm going to try and pin them down, but they are coming from three different directions, so it will be a challenge."

"Roger, 13 Golf. My boys will be there in 7 to 10 minutes. Hold on till then, and you will have some serious backup."

"Roger, Ron. I will keep the line open; here comes the first group."

The sound of gunfire filled the speakers in Ron's control centre. He turned to his 2IC, "Who is this guy? He has taken out 10 hostiles all by himself and rescued a whole town; at the moment it sounds like a Rambo remake."

The first stop group appeared, coming down Perranporth Hill from the Truro side, three in number, running down the road like they owned it or were just plain stupid. Stuart had a clear shot from his vantage point and tapped off three quick shots. Each one a hit. Each one a fatality.

The other two groups, one advancing down the hill from the Newquay side of town and the other from the Perrancoombe road, all slowed as they heard the fresh gunfire; and then took cover calling frantically on their radios.

An unknown voice broke through on their radio, "Welcome, boys. Advance to meet your destiny; your virgins in the sky await; your comrades have ALL gone before you. Come join them."

At that point the rifle in the hands of the old soldier cracked three times more – three shots, three hits, three fatalities – and the Newquay road group were no longer part of the equation. The air above Stuart's head came alive with the crack of passing bullets as the last group at last found his position and started to focus their fire, rather than just spraying it around as they had been doing.

Stuart hunkered down behind his wall for cover just as the sky above was filled with the sound of helicopters, and men in black combat suits rapelled down ropes to engage the last group of hostiles.

Stuart smiled to himself, "Looks like the cavalry in the form of 'The Regiment' has arrived at last." His job was done; the remaining hostiles were already throwing their weapons down in surrender.

Stuart leaned back against the wall, lifted his eyes to heaven and prayed, "Thank You, Lord, for Your miracle that took place here today. I acknowledge Your hand of strength, provision and protection. Please be with us all as we deal with the fallout. Amen."

CHAPTER THREE

Stuart rose slowly from behind the wall that had given him cover, held his hands high above his head, and lifted his voice and shouted, "13 Golf here, Ron's buddy. Don't shoot. Friendly."

A group of three black-clad, mean and fit-looking individuals broke away and made their way towards him. The tallest one spoke, "Confirm you are Stuart, 13 Golf?"

"That would be me," Stuart replied, a wry smile on his face. It was obvious the tall team leader was having trouble coming to grips with the fact that this short and slightly tubby guy, who had to be a least 50 years old, had been responsible for the very clean, clinical hits that had been made on the terrorists – each one downed with a single shot, each shot a killing shot.

Handing over his weapons Stuart said, "Glad to see you; things were getting tight. Shall we get the folk out of the supermarket?"

The tall team leader shook his head in amazement. From what he had seen, the remaining three terrorists would have been no match for this guy. *Who was he and what had he been up to before?*

Stuart shouted outside the door of the supermarket, "Tom. All clear; come out with the folks."

The door flew open and Tom burst out and ran across to his Dad, tears streaming down his face, "Dad, praise the Lord you are okay and that He was here today!"

Grabbing his Dad in a big bear hug that lifted him off his feet, he said, "You were amazing, appearing like you did; they were going to kill us all. I was about to try and jump them, at least go down fighting and perhaps give my family a chance to escape."

At the mention of family, Trish and Sam approached. Stuart embraced them and then, turning to the team leader, asked, "Can we get out of the public eye? I don't want to be identified or have my family marked for retaliation."

The black-clad team whisked Stuart and his family into a nearby surf shop, now standing empty. Once inside, Stuart helped himself to a pair of shorts and a shirt. "Be right back," he said as he headed to the facilities at the rear of the shop.

Ten minutes later he emerged, looking like a regular middle-aged holiday maker, all his kit in a large paper bag he had found.

Once again the team leader found himself gazing at this normal-looking guy in disbelief and wondering how he could have done what he did. Then he looked at the eyes, and he knew. Stuart's eyes were bright and full of intelligence, but also cold as steel. They were eyes that had seen much, eyes just like his and his men's, operator's eyes.

"Stuart, let's get you and your family out of here. My men are at your unit clearing out the dead terrorist and cleaning up. We would like to take you to one of our safe houses in Plymouth for debriefing."

"Fine with me, but what do I call you? Also, I need to let my wife know what's happening. She's at work in Truro; can you airlift her from there on the way?"

"Call me Alpha 1. Yes, we can pick her up on the way."

Stuart reached down for his trusty sat phone and made the call, 'Hi Jane, it's me."

The phone came alive with a million questions. News of the attacks was all over the media; 10 towns had been hit at the same time, and there were massacres in all of them except for Perranporth.

"Love, I'm fine; the kids are fine. We are coming to fetch you in a helo; be ready. I was in the thick of it and need to be debriefed, so we're being taken to Plymouth. Don't breathe a word to a soul about my involvement."

CHAPTER FOUR

Special Forces Safe House, Plymouth

The four military types sitting around the table gazed at the map and photos before them. The photos told the story of the Perranporth attack and the involvement of Stuart and Tom.

Looking across at Alpha 1, the crusty general said, "Okay, Joe, fill us in."

"Right, Sir. Stuart took out fourteen tangos; his son, Tom, took out two. Three were captured by our forces. It was the biggest team to hit any of the towns; the others ranged from eight to fifteen. Those who attacked the other towns all made clean getaways. So, we have about one hundred tangos still on the loose in the UK, if they have not fled. Of those killed in Perranporth, fifteen were British Nationals; all three captives are also British nationals, so we are looking at a major home-grown terror threat. To date we have established that 836 captives were slaughtered on live TV; that number may still rise as we sweep the areas involved. We now have major saturation of security forces on the ground."

The short concise report did not reflect the pain and terror that was gripping individuals, families and a nation. Panic and anger were high.

The general nodded, "Tell me about Stuart."

"Ex-Rhodesian Special Forces. Entered the army at 16, finished up at 21 as a Captain with the 3 highest awards for bravery. Nicknamed 'The Hulk' by his men. He spent the next 10 years doing high-level, very dangerous security work. He got married in that time and had two children – a daughter and a son. He then trained for the Christian ministry and has done that for more than 22 years. Moved to the UK 3 years ago; does conference speaking. His wife, Jane, is a nurse, and his son, Tom, is a Youth Worker. The daughter is married and living in South Africa, but plans to move here in 10 months' time.

"Here is an amazing thing. We gave him our operator's strategic intelligence test, and he scored 99% and broke the record for the quickest time by more than half. He has a military brain like a supercomputer."

The general's jaw dropped, "Say that again. 99% on the test? That's impossible!"

"No, Sir," Joe said. "99% is the mark, and he did it in record time."

"Joe," the general said, "we need to have this man on board; we need a mind like his in this war on terrorism."

"I agree," said Joe, "and he is not half bad in a fight as well."

Joe continued, "General, Stuart's been going over some more intelligence; he believes there is going to be another attack on the West Coast of Scotland. He heard the terrorists speaking about a town called Troon. Intel coming through seems to indicate that the terrorists responsible for the other attacks escaped out to sea in RIBs. Stuart believes that they had some sort of larger boat waiting for them."

The general's face creased with worry. "Do you mean that those madmen may now be closing in on some of the towns on the Scottish coast?"

"Yes, Sir," Joe replied. "I've ordered satellite images of the coast of Cornwall at the time of the attacks. It shows three fishing trawlers that were all within reach of portable boats; only one of them seems to be heading up the Scottish West Coast. I have Alpha, Bravo, Charlie and Delta groups ready to go."

"Roger. Do a forced insertion on the boat and see what we find. Let's plan to be over the target in less than two hours," commanded the general. "In the meantime, I will have a chat with Stuart."

Stuart looked up as the general walked in. "Hello, Sir," he said, as the general's steely eyes focused on him.

"You are quite an enigma," chuckled the general. "You have thrown my boys into a tizzy; they are really having a challenge trying to picture the fifty-something guy you are, doing what you did," smiled the general.

Stuart smiled and laughed, "To be honest, Sir, I'm having a challenge myself; it's a long time since I fired a shot in anger. All I can say is that God must have been with me and given me the strength that I needed. I mean, let's be real. Look at me: I'm short, fat and out of shape; what happened in Perranporth was a miracle!"

"Yes," the general said. "I agree that what happened in Perranporth was a miracle, but it was a miracle built on the skills that God had given you as a young man."

"Stuart", continued the general, "I need you. You have the sharpest military brain that we have ever seen, and I need you on my team. The fitness and fat we can work on, but I need your insights and strategic mind."

"General, I'm not sure," said Stuart. "I left that life behind me a long time ago."

"Stuart, there is an evil walking our country today, and I need you to be part of the team that will stop that evil. I, too, am a believer, but I need help – your help.

"I want to put in place a new unit – a unit that will have not only the necessary tactical skills, but also the spiritual insight to realise that it's not just bad guys we're dealing with, but also an unseen evil. Stuart, hear me out. Nearly all of the terrorists have been radicalised right here in the UK. They're home grown, and we don't know how many more there are. If we are not prepared, then many more may die; and I don't want that on my conscience. I don't believe you want it on yours either."

Stuart's face hardened. His eyes became like ice, as he remembered the fear and terror on the faces of the children and parents in the Perranporth square; the screams still echoed in his mind, and the look of sheer madness on the faces of the terrorists haunted him.

"General," said Stuart, "can I have a day to pray about it? I need to hear from God on this."

The general smiled. He knew what God's answer would be, and he knew that he had his man. "Come with me," said the general. "We have an op going down in an hour; we are going to drop in on that fishing trawler making its way up the Scottish West Coast."

CHAPTER FIVE

Temporary Operations Room
The Regiment's Safe House, Plymouth

In the operations room, the general and Stuart watched the scene taking place out in the Firth of Clyde unfold. The big screen showed a fishing trawler making its way through the choppy sea just as darkness was falling. From downwind came the sound of rotors as the Chinook helicopters carrying the four assault teams swept in.

As the helicopters appeared over the trawler, flickers of light began to erupt from the trawlers deck – small arms fire. The heavy machine guns on the Chinook helicopters opened fire, strafing the decks below them. Out of the open doors of the helicopter thick black ropes uncoiled, quickly followed by black-clad special force soldiers. Soon the deck below was full of small arms fire as the troops fought to gain a foothold.

Stuart watched the scene intently as the drama unfolded before him. "General," he said, "it looks like we have found this snake's nest".

The screen before Stuart and the general was alive with the flash of gunfire; Stuart's focus was still riveted to the screen. Suddenly, he swung round to the general and exclaimed, "Sir, get the troops off now! I believe that they're going to blow the boat rather than let it fall into our hands. That way they will also be able to kill a lot of our Special Force operators."

The general hesitated for just a moment then barked out an order into his headset, "Alpha 1, abort, abort, abort! I say again abort."

On the screen in the operations room men were seen scrambling up the ropes into the hovering helos. They had no sooner cleared the ship when a massive blast rocked the night sky; men still hanging onto ropes were swung violently from side to side as the helicopter pilots sought to regain control of their aircrafts.

"Stuart!" exclaimed the general. "How did you know that was going to happen?"

"Just a hunch, Sir," said Stuart. "Maybe God flagged it up for me. It just dropped into my mind that if they were putting up such a fierce fight, they didn't want to be taken prisoner; and perhaps the information on that ship was too valuable to fall into enemy hands."

Stuart continued, "General, what was the holding company of that ship?"

The operations room officer spat out that information. "The ship's name is the *Oily Mackerel*; it's registered to the Bounty Fishing Company right here in Plymouth."

"General," said Stuart, "we need to get a team there right now. Maybe they are innocent, but I doubt it; we need to stop them destroying any evidence that may assist us."

The general swung round and barked the orders out. Within minutes an assault team was making its way to the offices of the Bounty Fishing Company and the homes of the registered directors. Soon the radio came to life as the intel started to come in.

"Echo 1, Echo 1 to command 1. We have a warehouse full of arms and explosives and extremist literature. We have apprehended fifteen males and ten females who were on the premises."

"Roger that, Echo 1," said the general. "Secure the location, and bring the suspects in."

The general swung round to Stuart. "Well, my boy," he said, "you have done it again. Stuart, I need you on my team *now*."

"Sir, just give me the one day to pray it through," said Stuart.

"Okay, Stuart. You have one day, and one day only."

CHAPTER SIX

As the day unfolded more and more intel poured in, clarifying the picture. And the picture was frightening. The company held huge stockpiles of arms and explosives and had extensive plans to target soft targets all around the UK. A huge tragedy that could have occurred had been averted by one man's courage and determination to make a difference and to be available to God.

In their bedroom, Stuart and Jane were on their knees praying to God that He would give them the answer for the way forward. Tears poured down both their faces as they contemplated the future and grieved for the families that had lost loved ones.

Stuart turned to Jane, "Honey, I have to do this; it's not what I want, but I know it's what God wants."

Jane looked at her husband of 32 years and hugged him close saying, "Stuart, I love you, and I know that God will go with you. This is something you need to do to help rid us of this frightful evil that is sweeping the land."

"Right," said Stuart. "Let me go see the general and find out what he has to offer, what his plan is."

~~~~~
~~~~~

As Stuart entered the general's office, the old war horse behind the desk was smiling.

"You heard from God then, and He agreed with me."

"Yes, He did," said Stuart with a grimace on his face.

"Good," said the general. "Call me Rob now that we are going to be comrades. Stuart, here's the deal; you will be given the rank of general, will be answerable only to the Prime Minister, and will be given free rein to form your own unit. The unit's sole purpose will be to react to the threat that has arisen out of these attacks. The go-ahead has been given to recruit up to 500 men and women to form the unit."

"Right, Rob," said Stuart. "I would like to be based in Cornwall and use that area as a training ground."

"No problem, Stuart," Rob replied. "Consider it done."

~~~~~

Cornwall
Six months later

The lone figure stood on the hilltop looking down on the training camp that was nestled in the valley below. Images flashed before his eyes – the tears, pain and anguish of long runs, strict diets and hard physical training – pain that had borne its fruit. The
~~~~~

once tubby figure that had been Stuart was now transformed; a new slimmer, harder and fitter man had emerged from the despair and pain of the last six months.

Faces flashed before his eyes, the men and women who had been recruited to this elite unit. Each one was a born-again Christian. Each one was trained in the art of warfare. Each one stood ready to go to war against the forces of darkness in the form of the radicalised extremist Muslim element. They were an elite force of 300 men and women, forming four divisions of 75 each; with the designated call signs of Angels 1, Angels 2, Angels 3 and Angels 4, each division, led by a captain, was now ready and prepared to engage the enemy.

Stuart's mind drifted back to the recruitment of one of the young captains, his own son, Tom. The mental battle with himself was still with him. What father would send his son into a battle that could see him die? But Stuart's son, Tom, had insisted that he be allowed to join this unit. He had lost friends up and down the Cornwall coast in the terrorist attacks of six months ago. He too knew that now was the time that God needed men and women of character to stand in the breach and go out and do battle.

Stuart turned and made his way down the path that led to the parade grounds in the middle of the camp. There, men and women were gathering together into four distinct blocks. Angels 1 to 4 were preparing to go on parade, their lilac berets sporting the silver osprey of the newly formed unit, the

Special Assault Force or SAF. The men and women, drawn from all the different Armed Forces, shared one common denominator, their love for Jesus Christ. These men and women were ready to lay down their lives in the protection of the weak and the innocent and the land that they had come to love.

Stuart slipped into his office overlooking the parade ground and was quickly followed by a handsome young captain, Tom. Turning to face him, Stuart felt his eyes well up with tears – tears of pride, but also tears for the image of another young captain walking off a battlefield so many years ago.

Stuart found himself silently praying for all these young men and women – that they would be protected, and that the horrors of war would not scar them as it had so many others before them.

"Well, Tom, are we ready to go?" queried Stuart.

"Yes, Dad... I mean, Sir," Tom replied.

Stuart laughed. It was a challenge for Tom to remember that he was now talking to the general of an elite special force unit.

"Right, Tom, call the parade to order. I'll be out in a minute."

Stuart glanced across at his image in the mirror mounted on his office wall. A lean, sunburnt, determined face glared back at him under the lilac beret. "Job done," he thought. "Now I too am ready for battle."

Stuart turned and moved smartly out onto the parade ground, took his position behind the podium, and began his speech to the troops who stood before him.

"Today, we, the men and woman of the Special Assault Force, will go operational. There has arisen in our country a cancer that is eating the hearts and minds of innocent young people. That cancer, in the name of religion, is brainwashing them and forcing them to go out and do horrendous deeds against the innocent, against women, against children. The targets are the weak and defenceless.

"Our job, my Angels, is to wipe them off the face of the earth. It will not be easy, it will not be quick, it will not be pretty; but it is a job that must be done if we are to ensure that our children, wives and daughters can live in peace and safety. Therefore, take courage; be bold and let us put our trust in our Lord and King, Jesus Christ. Remember, it is for Him that we ultimately take up this task.

"Six months from now, some faces may well be missing. Any one of us could fall in battle. But remember this: because we have a personal knowledge and relationship with Jesus Christ, our reward is eternity with him. The Lord bless you all as you take up this great fight."

As the sounds of *The Last Post* broke out, Stuart straightened up, saluted the men and women before him, and then turned and made his way back to his office. Picking up the phone, he dialled a secure number and declared his unit open for business.

CHAPTER SEVEN

Inside the Sono Mosque in downtown London, the Imam slipped his eyes over the young men kneeling before him. Every one of them had been handpicked and radicalised by him; each one was prepared to die for him. In the heart of the Imam, Ishmael, burned a hatred of all things Western, and even more so of all things British.

He gave no thought to the fact that England had given him a home when, as a young refugee, he had arrived with his family from Pakistan. A home, benefits and many other things had been provided by the country he now hated. The stories of his grandfather, together with his radicalised teaching, had stripped away from the young, formative man who was to become the Imam, any love for England.

He now saw himself as the avenger, empowered by his god to wreak vengeance on the infidel nation and rescue his people from the trap of capitalism and Western culture. He hated with a passion the young women he passed on the street, dressed in their Western clothes, behaving like the infidel and flouting themselves before the true believers. He was consumed by hatred – a hatred that had matured and grown through the years, a hatred that no longer allowed him to see the young men before him as human beings, but rather just as tools to enforce his vengeance.

Ishmael's eyes narrowed as he ran through his next plan in his mind. It was a plan so daring, so many years in the making, that if successful would leave the nation that he hated so much reeling and in shock.

"Yes," he thought to himself, "my young fists are ready to do my bidding."

~~~~~

SAF Base, Cornwall

In his brand new office, Stuart looked up as the phone rang. Answering it, he acknowledged Rob on the other end.

"Hi, Rob. How are you doing?"

"I'm fine thanks, Stuart. I have some good news for you. The Queen wants to reward you for your bravery in Perranporth; she is going to award you a title, a very rare honour of a hereditary peerage, the Duke of Perranporth. In addition, your son, Tom, is to get an earldom, the Earl of Perranporth; and your daughter, Storm, will receive the title of the Countess of St. Ives. The Queen is also going to give you the Victoria Cross; Tom is to receive the George Cross."

Rob paused for a moment, expecting some comeback from Stuart, but only stunned silence greeted him over the phone line. Chuckling, he continued, "The Queen would like you to attend a banquet at the Lovet Country Estate in two weeks'
~~~~~

time. All of the country's top politicians and military minds will be there, and she would like you to meet them."

Straightaway, Stuart's mind started to race. "Rob, what about the security? That meeting would be an ideal opportunity for the extremists to strike."

"Stuart," replied Rob, "don't worry about that; we will have a full detachment of SAS on duty, and no one will be able to get past them."

Stuart pulled a wry face, "Rob, I just got another one of my hunches, and I need to ponder on it for a while."

"Don't worry, Stuart," said Rob. "I can assure you now; no one will be getting past my men. My SAS boys are the best."

"Right, Rob, touch base soon," Stuart said as he ended the call.

As soon as the phone was back on its hook, Stuart was out of his chair and moving through to his operations room.

"Bugs," he called out.

A tall, young captain turned round. Bugs, aka Captain Roy Franks, was a gifted intel and IT specialist. Roy was known to all as 'Bugs' because the huge horn-rimmed glasses he favoured seemed to magnify his eyes.

"What's up, Hulk?" he queried.

"I need to know everything there is to know about the Lovet Country Estate – history, building plans, the lot – and I need it all by tomorrow," Stuart commanded.

"Roger, Hulk," affirmed Bugs. "You will have it by 0800 hours tomorrow."

Moving back to his office, Stuart put out a call on the radio, "Angels 1, do you copy?"

Immediately the answer came back, "Roger that, Sunray. Angels 1 copies you fives."

"Right, Angels 1, get over to my office with all your section leaders," Stuart said.

"Roger, Sunray. Angels 1 on the way," Tom replied.

Thirty minutes later Stuart's office was filled with young men and women, the leadership team of the Angels 1 company.

"Right, listen up, you bunch. I've got some news and a hunch."

Stuart quickly brought them up to speed on the honours the Queen was going to award. This news was followed up with lots of applause and banter, Tom, the company commander of Angels 1, coming into more than his fair share. Rich, one of the young section commanders, started referring to him as 'Lord Dude', a name which was to stick.

"Settle down, you bunch," Stuart's voice cracked out. "I've got one of my hunches. This would be a perfect target for our extremists. The SAS is providing cover and protection, but I'm still uneasy; I want a mock-up of the estate on the practice range within two days, and I want to run every conceivable scenario."

All around the room heads nodded, and a low murmur broke out.

"Right. Get to it!" Stuart barked, and the room quickly emptied. Tom, however, lagged behind.

"What's up, Dad? You are looking stressed."

"Tom, or should I say *Lord Dude,*" said Stuart smiling, before his face turned serious. "I am stressed. I've got a really bad feeling about this; I feel sick to my stomach. Something is going to go down. I can feel the evil hovering, ready to attack."

Tom came up and put his arm around his Dad's shoulders, "Don't worry, Dad. God will lead and go before us. Is Storm flying in for the presentations?"

"That's part of the good news," said Stuart. "The government has granted them as a family immediate UK citizenship and is flying them over on an Air Force jet."

Tom grinned, "She will like that, no luggage restrictions."

Stuart laughed, "You had better watch out, young man. Special force operator or not, your big sister will still sort you out; she is a force to be reckoned with in her own right."

Tom grinned, "That she is, Dad. We had all better watch out!" He suddenly turned serious and asked, "How's Mom holding up under the pressure?"

"She is fine, Son," Stuart replied. "You know your mom, pure gold and a seriously strong woman, not to mention an awesome prayer warrior. She is coordinating the prayer backing we so desperately need." Stuart paused for a moment before adding, "Right, Son, let's get to it; we have work to do."

~~~~~

Stuart's bungalow on the Angels Base
Later that evening

The spider crept closer, its red eyes gleaming with hate and poison dripping from the large fangs. It shuffled along and then climbed onto a fist that seemed to sit on two rounded spheres, rocking to and fro. It suddenly reared up on its back legs and launched itself towards its target.

Stuart leapt out of bed, a shout dying on his lips. Switching on the light, his eyes scanned the room for the huge spider, but it was nowhere to be seen.

Jane raised her head off her pillow and grogglly asked, "What's wrong?"

"Just a bad dream," replied Stuart. At those words Jane sat bolt upright and wide awake.

"You only dream when God is trying to warn you of something very important. So what was the dream?"

Stuart quickly recounted the spider dream.

Jane's eyes crinkled up as she thought, "Well, the spider and fist are all pretty straight forward, but what on earth were the spheres?"
~~~~~

"I have no idea," mused Stuart, "but they must have some significance; it will be revealed in time. Let's get some sleep. Tomorrow will be a long day."

CHAPTER EIGHT

The Sono Mosque, Downtown London

Ishmael looked at the twenty-four young men before him; they represented years of planning. They were fit young men, each one of them in his prime. They had slipped into the mosque in the crowd there for the Friday prayers. Once inside they had quickly made their way to the secret room, their faces concealed by the large hoodies they wore. Once in the room the hoods fell back to reveal smart, young men with short hair, almost military in its cut. All were focused on Ishmael, the Imam, the fanaticism in his eyes reflected in theirs.

"My young fists," he said, "soon you will strike a blow that will send this nation crashing to its knees. Our successful raids in Cornwall have them living in fear. Now, we will show them that no one will be safe from us; we will show them that we can reach all levels and all places in our society. No one will be safe from the 'Fists' of the most high."

Pointing to a young man he said, "Sami will strike the first blow; then you, the rest of the fists, will arise and complete the devastation of this infidel nation. Are you ready to strike the killing blows for the most high?"

In unison the twenty-four gave their assent. Then, with Ishmael's blessing they rose and departed, hoods once more in place as they mingled with the departing crowds, making it impossible for the watching operatives from MI5 to identify them. The tide of extremist evil had been unleashed, and the havoc was just days away.

~~~~~

SAF Base, Cornwall

Stuart sat in his office talking to Rob, the SAS general.

"So, Rob, how many men are you deploying as cover for this banquet?"

Rob smiled, "I've got twenty-nine of my best men, led by a young lieutenant. Sam's been with the regiment for four years and has done outstanding work. Sam is a Muslim and has been a massive help in undercover work and tracking down extremists. The fact that we have Muslims in the regiment has really made the politicians happy – integrated society and all that stuff; they have all been outstanding and are experienced operators."

Rob grimaced before continuing, "I received serious pressure from the Home Office to ensure that a strong Muslim bias was included in the protection detail, flying the flag for tolerance and integration before all the bigwigs."

Stuart rocked back in his chair, a thoughtful look on his face. "Are you sure you don't want some of my Angels involved Rob?" he asked.
~~~~~

"Absolutely not, old boy. My lads from the regiment are very touchy and would take it as a personal slight if any of your boys were involved. Don't worry, Stuart; just enjoy the evening and remember you are coming out as a duke. Posh what!" said Rob with a chuckle in his voice.

"I don't feel posh, Rob, just concerned. I still have this niggle in my mind," replied Stuart.

"Stuart, chill," said Rob. "This time your niggle is just nerves at meeting the Queen. My chaps are on it and will make sure you are all safe."

"Right, Rob. See you on Saturday. Oh, by the way, when are your boys setting up?" Stuart asked.

"We arrive first thing on Saturday morning to do all the sweeps etc. See you then."

As Stuart put the phone down there was a thoughtful and pensive look on his face. Reaching for the radio he called, "Angels 1. Dude, Dude, this is Hulk. Do you copy?"

"Roger, Hulk. Dude here; reading you fives," came back Tom's reply.

"Right, Dude, get the leaders from Angels 1 in here stat," Stuart instructed.

"Roger, Hulk, on the way," Tom responded.

~~~~~
~~~~~

***Lovet Country Estate**
Saturday, 12 January 2013*

Lovet County estate was swarming with all sorts of security personnel – men and women from the police special protection services for the politicians, the Royal protection details for the monarchs, and the SAS. All around the estate men and women were setting up, making sure that the evening's proceedings would be as safe as possible.

~~~~~

Back in Cornwall at their SAF Base, Stuart was pacing up and down as Jane walked through from the bathroom and said to him, "Stuart, what's wrong?"

"I've just really got this niggle that something big is about to go down, and I have a huge amount of trepidation about tonight," said Stuart.

Jane looked lovingly across at her husband of 33 years and said, "You had the dream again last night, didn't you?"

Stuart looked at his wife with real love in his heart for her; the woman had stood by his side through thick and thin for so many years. He quietly said, "Yes, Love, I had the dream again last night, the same one – the spider, the fist and the two white spheres. I still can't get them out of my mind, what they are or what they signify. But I know beyond a shadow of a doubt that something big is about to break."
~~~~~

Jane came up and put her arms around her husband. She gave him a hug and a deep kiss and said, "Love, God is in control. He put us in Europe at this time at this place for a reason, just as He did with Esther. We will face it together, because we know that God is in control; and He is the God who always makes a way."

~~~~~

Later that evening Stuart, Tom and Storm together with Jane, Trish and Steve, Storm's husband, prepared for the meeting with the Queen. Stuart looked across at his young son in his best dress uniform, lilac beret and silver osprey gleaming. His gaze dropped to his son's chest; no medal ribbons yet, but after tonight it would sport the ribbon of the George Cross.

Stuart looked across at his own reflection in the mirror, and it showed that on his breast were just four medal ribbons, dating back to a country not remembered by many, forgotten in the annals of history by most – a country once called Rhodesia, but now known as Zimbabwe.

Displayed on Stuart's chest were the ribbons of the Grand Cross of Valour, the Silver Cross, the Bronze Cross and the General Service Medal. Four simple medals, but medals that told a tale of great courage and a high degree of action and violence and involvement in a bloody war.

Stuart called his family together and said, "We don't have much time, but whatever happens
~~~~~

tonight, I want you to know that I love you all and that am proud of you all. Don't forget we have a God who cares and loves us; God has put us in a privileged position for such a time as this, just as He did with Esther. We need to trust Him in every single aspect and know that we can be the people God intended us to be, to be able to just do what He wanted us to do here in this place."

Stuart gathered them all together. They joined hands, and he prayed a simple prayer, "Lord, today, please be with us. Put your hand of protection upon us and watch over us. Keep us and help us to be the men and women that you decreed us to be. Thank you, Jesus; we exalt Your name. Amen."

~~~~~

Soon the halls of Lovet County Estate were abuzz with politicians and dignitaries, members of the Royal family mixing together with different military and civilian types.

Rob, the SAS general, came up and tapped Stuart on the shoulder and said, "Stuart, it's time; the Queen is here, and they are waiting for us in the main ballroom."

Stuart looked across at Tom, nodded his head and led his family as together they made their way to the main hall.

The monarch, Queen Elizabeth the Second, smiled as they bowed, acknowledging her status as the leader of the United Kingdom. The Queen, with
~~~~~

her many years of experience and with a graciousness honed in her special privileged position, slipped into the ceremony that would give Stuart and his family the honours she had decided on.

After the short ceremony there was a lot of clapping and shaking of hands. People came up and offered their congratulations to all.

Stuart, although enjoying himself, still had a feeling of unease; he looked across at Rob and quickly made his way across to him.

"Rob, what's the status of your guys outside?" Stuart asked.

"I had a short message from them just a few minutes ago, but if you want I could call again." Rob reached out and touched his throat mike as he called out, "Keepers 1, Keepers 1, do you copy? Keepers 1, Keepers 1, do you copy? This is Eagle 1."

No reply came back over the radio and a furrow formed on Rob's brow. "Keepers 1, Keepers 1, do you copy?" Silence.

Rob tried once again, "Keepers 1, do you copy?"

The silence hung like a great white shark poised to attack, a cold chill forming in both Rob and Stuart's hearts.

Then, a very weak voice came across at the other end of the radio, "Eagle 1, Eagle 1, this is Keeper 2. Have been shot; green on green. I say again, green on green." And then the voice faded.

A look of absolute horror crossed Rob's face; green on green meant that the sergeant major assigned to the protection detail had been shot by some of his own men.

As Stuart heard those words and saw the look on Rob's face, he in turn reached up and touched the throat mike which had been concealed below the neckline of his collar and put in a call, "Angels, fly. Angels, fly. Angels, fly. This is a go. Angels, fly. Angels, fly. Please be aware, all Keepers call signs are now hostile. Hulk out."

Stuart swiftly moved across the room to the Queen and the Royal family, collecting Jane, Storm and Steve, and Tom and Trish on the way. On reaching the Queen he said, "Your Majesty, we have a security complication."

At his words some of the members of the Queen's protection detail closed very quickly around them. "Please follow me," said Stuart. They all moved quickly from the main reception hall into an ante-room, Stuart making his way towards a huge, ornate mantelpiece. Sliding his hands across the top of the mantelpiece, he pushed the first, third and sixth nodules of wood inward. Suddenly, the whole mantelpiece started to rotate revealing a secret door.

Stuart quickly moved the Royal family, together with his family, through the door and into a huge room on the other side, a hide-away that very few knew about but that had come up in Bugs' research. Stuart's men had furnished the room the day before in case they had need of it, and the group now settled into the comfortable seats.

Stuart spoke to the Royal family, "Please, Your Majesty, stay here together with your protection detail."

Stuart then turned to Jane, and dropping a hurried kiss on her lips, he said, "Hon, you and the rest of the family stay here with the Queen and her men." Stuart and Tom then slipped back through the secret door, closing it behind them.

As they moved through the door, both Stuart and Tom reached down and from an ankle holster pulled out their Sig Sauer P239- 9 mm pistols. Stuart moved very, very quickly towards the man-bag that he had brought with him, lifted out two pairs of night vision goggles and passed one pair to Tom. Stuart was pretty confident that in the next few minutes the lights would go out, and they would become a target for a full-scale assault. At that same time, the protection forces for the different politicians were moving in and starting to move the high-profile targets back from the doors and windows.

Simultaneously, four secret panels also opened up in different parts of the house, and out of them poured men and women dressed in black assault suits with a lilac patch bearing the image of an Osprey on the sleeve.

They were the Angels. They had been secreted into the building the day before, long before the other security personnel had arrived. Earlier in the week, Stuart had had Bugs go through the blueprints and family history of Lovet Hall; Bugs had discovered a secret passage and a number of secret rooms within Lovet that perhaps not even the current owners knew about. Stuart had moved his teams in early to make sure that they were positioned to proceed and intervene if needed.

At that moment all sorts of things were running through Stuart's mind; however, more pressing matters were at hand as the windows exploded inward, the lights went out and dark figures leapt through the gaping holes. People started to scream and run in all different directions, but Stuart and his crew of Angels were locked in heavy contact with the dark figures that had invaded the rooms. Stuart, now in possession of an automatic weapon one of his men had thrown him, opened fire. All around the sound of suppressed gunfire mingled with the sounds of shots taking effect as they hit human flesh. For a few minutes there seemed to absolute pandemonium; smoke began to fill the room, wafting in the pitch darkness.

Then, as if someone had flicked a switch, there was absolute silence, followed by the soft whimpering of some of the guests.

The radio came alive as the different Angels sections called in their sit-reps. A mere six minutes had elapsed, but it was all over.

Stuart quickly made his way to the panel where all the lighting was controlled, stepping over the body of the security operative who had been assigned to guard it. The neat bullet hole in his head was a clear indication as to why he had failed at this task.

Stuart flicked the main control switch back up, while pulling off his NVGs. Looking around, he surveyed the scene of absolute mayhem. There were a few guests down, hit by stray bits of glass when the windows had been blown in. Crumpled on the floor all around the perimeter were a number of bodies – men dressed in black overalls and wearing night vision goggles.

Stuart moved across to the bodies sprawled in the different positions of men who had taken hits and died. He approached the one who'd been in the lead, pulling off his black balaclava to reveal the face of the young SAS lieutenant, Sam – or Sami as he was called by the Imam, Ishmael. Sam had taken a shot clean between the eyes; one of the young Angels, or perhaps even Stuart or Tom, had made the killing shot. It was difficult to say in the heat of the battle, but a clean, precise shot had taken down this young SAS traitor.

Stuart turned around to see Rob. The SAS general's face was ashen, and his hand held his left shoulder as he sank to the ground. He had taken a hit. Fortunately, it looked to be a through and through, too high to have done any major damage to vital organs, but still a vicious body blow. Stuart called out, "Medic, Medic, I need Angels medics up here right now."

As the medics moved across to Rob, the general slipped down onto the floor, eyes locked on the face of his now dead SAS lieutenant, Sam.

Rob looked across at Stuart as the medics began to work on him, "I don't understand it; he was one of my best men."

Stuart moved across to the other slumped figures, all of them SAS men. He reached down to pull off the balaclavas revealing that every single one of them was a young Asian man with a military haircut. Stuart turned to Rob, and with a look of sadness on his face reluctantly surmised, "Rob, this is what I feared. I think this is what God has been trying to warn us about; these young men have been radicalised, and they have deeply infiltrated what is deemed the most elite unit in the UK. They earned your trust in a big way, all the while waiting for their moment."

As Stuart's medics continued to work on Rob, Stuart heard the reports coming in from his Angels in different parts of the grounds. "This is Angels 1. We have secured the perimeter, but unfortunately we have four deceased... I say again, four deceased SAS personnel, non-Asian. It appears they were taken out by their own men. Keeper 2 is still alive, but he's in really bad shape; the medics are with him now."

Once Stuart received that call, he moved across and pushed the modules in the fireplace in the same sequence as he had before. The secret entrance flew open revealing again the Monarch and the Royal family, together with Stuart's own family. All of them looked horrified. They had heard the sounds of shooting and the things that were going on. Stuart went straight across to the Queen and said, "Your Majesty, it's all taken care of, but I think we need to get you back to the palace as quickly as possible. We have a lot of work to do here and we need to make sure that you are safe."

At that point more security officers from the monarchy detail swarmed into the room and began to usher the Royal family towards the grand door, their vehicles waiting outside ready to whisk them away to safety. The Queen stopped in mid-stride and turned towards Stuart saying, "Please convey to all my forces my very deepest appreciation for the bravery they have shown here tonight. I am immensely touched by their courage and dedication."

Stuart brought his hand up in a smart crisp salute and replied, "Yes, Ma'am, as you wish."

As Stuart watched the Queen depart, he was once again amazed by this remarkable, graceful lady who was their Queen. In the midst of the mayhem of the evening she still projected the quiet, steadfast strength that made her such a very special lady.

Stuart approached Jane, "Don't worry! We're all okay, but we will be very busy for the next few hours with the mop up and debrief." He once again reached down to touch the mike on his throat and said, "Angels 1, Angels 1, can I have Calamity Jane, please?"

A few minutes later a young Special Force female operative walked through the door. Calamity Jane was her call sign. Stuart detailed Calamity to take Jane and his family to a place of safety. "Take your section with you. Make sure they are safe for the rest of the evening; in fact, take them back to the base by helo."

Major mop-ups were underway; more SAS men started to pour in as The Regiment came to terms with their biggest betrayal ever. Stuart's mind was racing, already trying to piece together the things that had happened.

Stuart and Tom made their way through to the room that had become the temporary mortuary. It was a holding place for the body bags of those men who had been SAS, men who had turned on their own and sought to deliver a lethal blow by taking out the monarch and a number of leading politicians. As Stuart looked down the row of body bags, twenty-four in all, he turned round to see Rob, who had resisted going to the hospital to get his wound treated. Rob had allowed the medics to deal with his wound on-site, but was still walking around with an ashen face trying to come to terms with this absolute betrayal. It was something The Regiment had never encountered before, something which had rocked him to the very foundations of everything he believed in. Stuart turned to him and said, "Rob, something's just hit me."

Moving across to the first body bag, Stuart opened it to reveal the face of the young lieutenant who had been called Sam. Stuart turned the body over and pulled down the back of his battledress to reveal the cleft of his buttocks, close to where the spine ended. Stuart took his fingers and slowly spread open that little cleft of the buttocks; there, nestled between those two half-moons, was a tattoo of a spider – a red spider enclosed by a fist. Suddenly, it all made sense to Stuart. Suddenly, he knew exactly what the dream that God had given him meant.

Stuart turned to Rob saying, "Come over here. Have a look at this."

Rob moved across and Stuart showed him the tattoo very cleverly concealed in the cleft of Lieutenant Sam's buttocks. Stuart moved across to the next body bag and opened and checked that soldier, then the one next to him, until he had checked them all. Every single one of them had the same tattoo, neatly hidden in the same obscure location. If nobody knew they were there, they would never have had a chance of being seen. But each one of them told the tale of a dark extremist brotherhood.

Stuart turned to Rob again, "I believe what we have here is the tip of iceberg. If these chaps could infiltrate your unit, the very best this land can offer, then we have a problem. I just have this deep gut feel that there are more of them, and that they've infiltrated our Armed Forces in every single department. We need to act now. We need to act decisively. Let's get the command group together; we need to start moving."

Stuart and his team moved rapidly, setting up a temporary command post in the Lovet Country Estate's main building.

Stuart felt deeply grieved at the deaths that had taken place that evening. He realised that they were dealing with a major insurgence, a covert operation that had perhaps been years in the making, and that may have resulted in the infiltration of every level of the Armed Forces of the United Kingdom.

Stuart got on the radio and asked to be patched through to Number 10 Downing Street, the home of the United Kingdom's Prime Minister, David Cribbs. Well aware of the fact that it was only 3am, Stuart still felt compelled to make the call – even if it meant waking the nation's leader.

As Mr Cribbs came on the line, Stuart said, "Good morning, Sir, the Duke of Perranporth here. We need to have a meeting, and it needs to be immediate. What we've uncovered here tonight from the intel that we have been able to gather so far shows that we are actually in a position of major national crisis, and I need to see you right now. We can bring a helicopter across to drop me off, together with one or two of the other command officers."

From the tone of the voice on the other end of the line, Stuart could tell that David Cribbs was in deep shock at what had gone down at the Lovet Estate. It had rocked him. "Get here as soon as you can, Stuart," said David. "We need to discuss this and deal with the fallout as quickly as we can."

Stuart turned to address the other command leaders, "I want you to mobilise all Angels; we need everybody on standby, everybody ready to go. Make sure that they've got their go-bags. I think we are going to have a frantic forty-eight hours."

Stuart and Rob, accompanied by Joe, the SAS major, moved across to the helicopter and clambered in. The pilot lifted off straightaway, and in the matter of seconds the command group found themselves being whisked over the dark English countryside. The bird was soon landing not very far from Number 10 Downing Street.

Once clear of the helicopter's rotors, the group was met by one of the Prime Minister's aides and ushered through a side door and into an office, where David Cribbs waited for them.

Stuart looked to Mr Cribbs and said, "Sir, we need to talk privately — just you, me and the men that I brought with me."

David nodded to his aide. "It's alright, John. I'll call you again as soon as I need you."

After the aide had departed, Stuart turned to the Prime Minister and briefly outlined what they had discovered with the spider tattoo. "Sir, I believe what we are dealing with is a major infiltration at every single level of our forces, possibly in every single unit of the army, police, civil service, and who knows where else... There could be a secret army just waiting to arise right within our very borders. Sir, this is the greatest threat that we are facing since the Second World War."

Mr Cribbs looked across at Stuart, and Stuart could see that he was actually bowled over by what was unfolding, not quite sure what to do. "Any suggestions, Stuart?" he asked.

"Sir, we have to try and negotiate this crisis; but with our current legislation and the whole issue of human rights, it could prove to be a nightmare. We could end up bogged down in the red tape and bureaucracy and give the enemy forces the time they need to escape."

Looking Mr Cribbs in the eye Stuart continued, "What we need, Sir, is for you to declare martial law; we need to mobilise all the troops we know we can trust, and at this stage there may be precious few of them. Then, we need to lock down all our military bases and police units, and we need to get our trusted units in there combing through all of our personnel, grabbing hold of those that we find with this identifying tattoo.

"Once that's done, we need to step up the sweep to include mosques, universities, schools, politicos and every level of our society. We must ensure that we sweep up as many radicals in the first sweeps as we can.

"Sir, we also need to close our borders. If our borders remain open, they can run like rats; and with the free movement in the EU zone, they could be across the border within hours. After taking refuge in France, Germany... or any European country for that matter, they would be able to return to the UK whenever they feel it is once again safe to do so.

"So, essentially... we need to close our borders − nobody in, nobody out for the next 48 hours – and declare martial law. And we need to do it now!"

David Cribbs' mind was clearly reeling from what Stuart had just suggested. He turned and asked, "Is there no other way?"

Rob then jumped into the conversation. "Sir, I agree with Stuart. This is the only way to go. We need to move now, and we need to move decisively if we want to have any hope of dealing with this threat."

David Cribbs looked across at the three men, weighing the pros and cons. What could this do to his political career? How would it impact the future of his party? But ultimately, he realised that as Prime Minister the safety of the nation rested in his hands, and he had to make a decision – a decision which may not be popular, but a decision which had to be made regardless.

One hour later, the press were clamouring at Number 10 Downing Street as David Crlbbs came out and made a statement.

"As of 05:00 hours today, the United Kingdom is under a state of national emergency. I have declared martial law, putting certain elements of the military in absolute command. We have suspended some of the laws within our constitution as outlined in the martial law policy, and for the next 48 hours we have sealed our borders."

Hands shot up all over. "Mr Prime Minister, why is this necessary? What has happened to prompt such drastic action?"

David Cribbs looked towards the reporters and the TV cameras that were focused on him, and said, "Last night, at the Lovet Estate, there was a deadly attack – a deadly attack against Her Majesty, Queen Elizabeth, the Royal family, and the politicians attending the event held there." David Cribbs paused like the good politician he was; then, speaking into the stunned silence he said, "The tragedy of the whole incident was that the perpetrators were men and women of our own Armed Forces, men and women who had been put into positions of trust to protect us. In actual fact those in this privileged position of trust turned out to be the enemy."

The shockwave that rippled through the reporters was almost palpable; this was almost unprecedented. One reporter shouted out, "Any casualties, Sir? Is the Queen alright? Is the Royal family safe?"

David Cribbs gave a wide wry smile; nobody asked if any of the politicians were alright, which more or less showed what they thought of politicians. "Her Majesty and the Royal family are all safe, thanks to the very speedy intervention of another special force unit. This unit is not highly publicised and is only recently formed; it answers directly to me."

David Cribbs gave another wry smile; this would score him some brownie points in the polls, he hoped. Mr Cribbs continued, "The unit was formed seven months ago after the Cornwall attacks. It was formed specifically to deal with UK home insurgencies; and due to their heroic actions last night, this attack was foiled. Unfortunately, all of those involved in perpetrating the attack were killed, so we were not able to gather any valuable intel about the source of the attack. However, I can confirm that the attackers were members of another elite special force unit of the UK Armed Forces."

Hands again shot up all over, and questions were fired at Mr Cribbs. The Prime Minister looked across the group and said, "At this moment in time, for reasons of national security, I cannot answer any more of your questions. But I will keep you informed as this situation unfolds. Thank you very much for your time. Have a good day, and we will speak again this evening."

At that, Mr Cribbs turned and disappeared through a side door as he made his way back to where Stuart, Rob and Joe were waiting. "Generals," David said, "it's done. Over to you now; do what you need to do to ensure that this nation of ours is secure."

CHAPTER NINE

Back at the briefing room at the SAF base in Cornwall, Stuart was standing before the different divisions of the Angel Group. Angels 1 to 4 were joined by a unique group of SAS handpicked men, men that had been checked and cleared as not having the tattoo.

"Right, ladies and gentlemen," Stuart said, "we have to move fast. We will be breaking you up into units of five, made up of both men and women. The units will consist of both Angels and SAS. You will be moving to every military base; these bases have been locked down, and all military personnel have been recalled from leave. We need to do a physical check on every single soldier, every single contractor, and every single civilian that is involved with the Armed Forces of the United Kingdom. We will do this for the Army, Air Force and Navy. We've got people on board the different ships who are already starting to carry out this particular operation. Anybody that is found to have the tattoo will be arrested on the spot and taken into custody.

"Captain Flavell has your assignments. Once you have received them, you will need to move fast. We don't have a lot of time, so we need to move decisively."

Stuart then called across to Angels 4. "Sections 1, 2, 3, 4 and 5, I need you to remain behind. I have another assignment for you."

Stuart gathered Angels 4 around him. "My briefing to you is as a result of something Rob mentioned. There was immense pressure put on him to have a high number of Asian SAS troops involved in the detail that was meant to provide protection at Lovet House. When I asked him where that pressure came from, he said it was from one of the joint committees on defence. That committee is chaired by one of the Asian MPs; your task is to move in and physically check every single politician. They will most likely scream and shout and demand their rights, but just remind them that those rights have been suspended, because we are in a state of martial law. I need you to go through every MP and every politician. Those found with that particular tattoo will likewise be taken into custody, understood?"

Men and women nodded. "Right, let's get to it; we have 48 hours to get it wrapped up. After that, the rats will be running like crazy. Let's get going."

Stuart moved across to the operations room and stuck his head around the door. "Bugs," Stuart called. His logistics and IT Captain swung round.

"Yes, Sir?"

"First of all, Bugs, great job in getting those blueprints and the intel on Lovet for us. It made all the difference; I really commend you, Bugs," Stuart said.

Bugs' face beamed; it felt good to know that he had been part of thwarting such a decisive blow from the enemy. Even though he was not a front-line combat soldier, he was still able to make a monumental difference in the fight.

"Right, Bugs, another assignment for you now. We can't house all the people we will be arresting; I believe – if my hunch is correct – that the numbers could run into the thousands. We can't place them in a prison, where they could have an effect on somebody else, so I need you to scour the United Kingdom for me. Find me a place that is remote; find me a place that has the capacity to hold thousands of prisoners in complete isolation, a place that is excessively difficult to get to. Don't worry if it's not the Ritz; it doesn't matter if it's not two or three star accommodation, as long as we can fit people in there and keep a reasonable watch on them. And, Bugs... you've got less than an hour to get this done."

<center>~~~~~</center>

Stuart sat at his desk, together with Rob and Joe. They heard the calls start to come in as the different detachments reached their points of operation, taken there by fast attack helicopters. Once on-site, each group began to carry out the first phase of their mission, that of identifying those within the Armed Forces of the United Kingdom who were actually terrorists and traitors. As the reports began to come in, it soon became obvious that there had been a mass infiltration into the UK's Armed Forces; some units were presenting an especially high percentage of men and women bearing the identifying tattoo. The magnitude of the problem literally grew with every hour.

Bugs popped his head through the door and said, "Sir, I've found a place for you."

Stuart ushered him in. "Okay, Bugs, give it to us."

Bugs approached the big computer screen on the wall and touched it; up flicked a picture of the United Kingdom, and he pointed to an island at the top end of Scotland's Outer Hebrides.

Bugs explained, "On that particular island there is a prison. It's an underground prison that was mothballed about ten years ago. There's been a small crew there, just to keep the damp out and ensure the place is secure. The powers that be thought that we might have to use it again one day. It's highly inaccessible, and we can house up to 10,000 people there. They will literally be crammed in like sardines, but it is remote and secure."

Stuart turned round and said, "Okay, tell me about access."

"We have access from the air and sea," Bugs said. "There is a natural port, which can take three to four big fishing trawlers."

Stuart assessed the information, then said, "Right, I want a company of our guys up there. I need at least a hundred men who will be able to act as guards."

Continuing, Stuart turned to the SAS officers, "We're already stretched. Will your boys be able to provide eighty percent of the logistics we need?"

Rob looked across at Stuart with a steely grin in his eye as he ran the events of the past hours through his mind. "You had better believe it, Stuart," he affirmed. "We can get back at those guys who sought to undermine us as a Regiment. We've taken a hit, but we don't stand back for anybody. Yes, we will do whatever you need, and I'm pretty sure that once we've cleared some of the Royal Marines, we will be able to draw from them as well. As you know, we are all going to be pretty stretched with what's unfolding."

~~~~~

The next 48 hours across the United Kingdom saw a high level of activity; police, army, and politicians were all checked. Teams of military men and women swept into universities and colleges, swept into mosques, swept into estates and schools, checking people for the tattoo. Sweeps into the NHS and civil service followed, the number of tattoo-marked people climbing exponentially.

Stuart, sitting in his Ops Room with Rob and Joe, saw the numbers grow like a major tsunami sweeping in as more and more reports came in. It soon became evident that Stuart's hunch was more than a hunch; what they had uncovered at Lovet House was merely the tip of the iceberg.
~~~~~

It was obvious that this plan had been put in place years before. It was a well-thought out plan – a plan of infiltration, a plan for sleepers to lie quietly until they were mobilised to attack the land that had provided food, education and shelter for them.

Stuart turned to Joe and said, "Well, at last count we have been able to identify over eight thousand people with the tattoo. Of those, six and a half thousand men and women have come out of our Armed Forces. That is a significant number. And we're talking about people who were involved in every single sector, including those sectors dealing with nuclear power. They had the capacity to cripple us as a nation, if they had all mobilised at the same time and put their plan into action. I believe that was the plan, that there would be an uprising that would cripple and immobilise us and literally bring us as a nation to our knees, making us vulnerable to attack from all sorts of different groups. Right, I think it's time to go and brief the Prime Minister in person."

~~~~~

Stuart, Rob and Joe found themselves back at Number 10 Downing Street. As they walked into the Prime Minister's personal office, they saw Mr Cribbs sitting at his desk. He was looking haggard; dark rings shadowed his eyes. It was evident that he, too, had been taking quite a battering from the press. Different human rights groups, and first ministers and presidents within the EU zone were all
~~~~~

screaming and shouting and complaining about closing the borders of the United Kingdom for the 48 hours. Yes, the Prime Minister had taken his fair share of the battering.

Mr Cribbs beckoned the three men to sit down. As they settled into the comfortable seats in the Prime Minister's office, Stuart began his situation report, "Sir, the numbers are huge. We are looking at people in excess of eight thousand, six and half thousand of them from within the Armed Forces of the United Kingdom. Within our own politicians, we have identified thirty-five MPs, elected officials who were sitting on all different types of committees that form part of this conspiracy. We found them in education, we found them in our judges, and we found them in our police force; in every single strata of society we found them. Sir, I believe that we need to take even further decisive actions."

The Prime Minister looked across at Stuart, seeming almost reluctant to ask for an explanation to Stuart's comment. "More decisive action?" he asked with trepidation in his voice.

Stuart looked Mr Cribbs firmly in the eye and answered, "Yes Sir, more decisive action is needed." He paused a moment to gauge Mr Cribbs' reaction before continuing, "Sir, I believe that we need to withdraw from the European Union. We need to suspend our membership and the free movement across our borders with immediate effect. We've dealt a major blow to this Islamic extremist movement that sought to undermine and to bring this wonderful nation of ours into a place where it would be shattered and broken; but in order to prevent a repeat, we need to protect our borders.

This means we have to stop the leaky borders we have; we have to check every single person coming in and coming out of the nation. We need to be in a position where we can stop them at our borders and turn them back, Sir. Unfortunately, as long as we remain part of the EU, and we hold to all the treaties and the free flow of men and women back and forwards we are vulnerable.

Those that we've missed in the first swoop of the net − and there will be some − can seek to exit the country; others will seek to come in to take their place. And who knows what else will come, Sir? We have to do this if we are to win this battle."

Mr Cribbs realised that this was a defining moment in both his and the country's history. Failure to complete the task would leave the UK exposed and open to a higher level of risk. He looked across at Stuart, Rob and Joe and said, "Okay, gentlemen. I've trusted you this far, and it's come up trumps. Yes, I've taken a real drubbing from the press, but the polls out there are saying that with the man and woman in the street my shares have risen dramatically. At last they're calling me a leader who is prepared to act decisively and take whatever steps are necessary for the good of the nation."

He continued, "I will do it. I'll call a press conference and announce that I am going to invoke my Prime Minister's special powers with immediate effect. We are also going to extend the state of emergency for another 72 hours to give you the time you need to complete the work you need to do."

~~~~~

The Sono Mosque, Downtown London

The Imam was down on his knees in the secret room trying to come to terms with the things that had happened in the last 48 hours. Years and years of planning, years and years of work had been shattered and broken. He couldn't understand it; how could his young 'Fists' have failed? They had been the very best soldiers in the country, men put in place and tasked to infiltrate the most elite military unit. He couldn't understand how they could have failed; something must have gone radically wrong.

What the Imam failed to take into account was the fact that there is a God, the God of the Hebrews and the born-again believer. And this God most High was watching over the United Kingdom – not because it was a Godly nation, because it wasn't – but because of the prayers of a small number of genuine believers who cried out to Him daily.

And God was working through a small group of men and women who had committed their lives to him – the small group of men and women who made up the Special Assault Force, the 'Angels' that God had put in place to be the physical hands and feet on
~~~~~

the ground to stop this rising force of wickedness and evil that was seeking to bringing its own brand of oppression, violence and mayhem. An evil that was seeking to bring a nation into suppression under the extreme radical Islamic laws that would have robbed people of their freedom, of all their rights.

Ishmael had failed to include God in the scene as he was planning. And as a result, his plan had failed. He had failed. He just sat where he was and shook his head, as he mentally tried to come to terms with everything he had lost.

Suddenly, from the front of the mosque came the loud noise of a disruption. The sound continued from the back and sides of the building, as Special Force units swept into the mosque and began to round up the people who were there. The Imam, watching what was happening through CCTV, was confident they would not find him in the secret room. As soon as the borders were open again, he would flee the country and make his way across to Syria. Once there, he would begin to meet with the other commanders that made up the elite cell of leaders. From there they would regroup and plan their next phase of attack.

As Ishmael sat there calculating his next steps, he heard the sound of electric power saws outside. What was going on? Suddenly, the walls began to vibrate. "No! It's not possible; they could not know I was here. No one knew. No one would betray me."

What Ishmael had failed to consider was that modern security forces had thermal imaging resources, and his image and heat signature had been picked up clearly on the sophisticated equipment. Within seconds, the soldiers broke through the wall and took Ishmael into custody. He would soon join the growing number of people on a remote island in Scotland, where he too would be held to account for the deeds that he had planned.

CHAPTER TEN

It was five days after the Lovet House attack. On a remote island at the very extreme edge of the Outer Hebrides, helicopters were dropping from the sky with monotonous regularity, offloading men and women dressed in bright orange prison garb. Hands and legs were shackled together as they shuffled their way down to the cells. The number was growing with every passing minute. Soon, they would have in excess of nine thousand people.

Stuart stood on the shores of the small island, his eyes scanning the whole time. Looking around, he turned to Rob who was standing next to him and commented, "Right, if there is going to be a rescue attempt – and I believe they will try, because there is no way that the Muslim commanders are going to allow so many of their choice people to be picked up and interrogated – we need to be prepared. They probably know that we only have a small force to guard this place. Yes, the chances of a rescue attempt are really strong, and we need to be ready."

Rob turned to Stuart and said, "Stuart, what's your feeling on when they will try?"

"I think they will attempt it within the next 24 hours. They cannot allow more time than that; they will know we need to start interrogating the prisoners. And they cannot allow us the time that we need to build up our force here once we are done with the initial sweeps. They have to act soon.

"I'm sure they have access to satellite resources from nations sympathetic to them and are already observing overhead. Somehow or other, they *will* get Intel. Though we have swept up a lot of their people, I'm pretty sure there are still some in hiding. Some of those we haven't been able to get to may have log-in protocols and could even be monitoring our communication; we are still very vulnerable, and we need to be ready for anything.

Rob nodded his head and added, "We are so thinly spread on the ground. Unfortunately, at the moment our forces are deployed in so many different areas right across the region – Ireland and Northern Ireland, right up north into Scotland, and down south in England and Wales. With our forces so thinly spread, we just can't put a big force here; we can only just manage a company of 120 personnel.

Stuart agreed, "With this growing number of people, it's going to become a logistical nightmare to guard them over the next 48 hours. If the enemy does come, we will have the fight of our lives on our hands, so we need to be ready."

Stuart turned, and together with Rob and Joe, made his way across to a waiting helicopter. They jumped on board; and as they lifted off and the island below faded from the view, Stuart had a real premonition of darkness and death hovering over the island, just waiting to explode into violence again.

~~~~~
~~~~~

The guards that were on duty wearing their night vision goggles picked up some movement down on the beach. Sure enough, a deeper inspection would have shown that four freighters had quietly made their way into the bay below and were right now disgorging their cargo of men, men draped in shemagh head coverings and armed with AK-47s and RPG rockets. The insurgents were making their way silently up the beach, as they headed towards the fortified gates of the makeshift prison.

Suddenly, the night sky lit up as an RPG-7 rocket arced through the sky and made contact with the front doors of the prison. The doors buckled from the pressure of the tremendous blast, but didn't give. The walls around the prison came alive as the men and woman of the guarding group opened fire on the figures scrambling up on from the beach below. Making their way – weaving, ducking and diving – the figures moved forward all the time. There must have been at least four hundred, possibly even five hundred, Jihadi warriors moving up towards the gates of the prison.

With the crackle of fire all around, the guard group's radio came alive with Stuart's voice, "Hulk to Angels 4, do you copy?"

"Angels 4 here. We copy."

"Roger, Angels, I need you out. Retreat. Pull back; pull back. The forces that you're facing are too large for you to contain or defend against. We've got them visual on satellite; they are just too big a group for you to hold. Pull back. Pull back. There are helicopters waiting in the square; get on board and pull back, Angels 4. We will try other means to attempt to restrain the situation."

The order quickly passed between the mixed group of SAS and SAF operatives. They pull backed and made their way to the helicopters that were waiting for them. Scrambling aboard, they were quickly lifted up into the dark night sky. The helicopters showed no navigational lights and were quickly swallowed up in the darkness.

The night sky lit up again with flashes as another barrage of RPG-7 rockets hit the prison gates, blowing them open. Through the now open gates streamed a horde of men dressed in their shemaghs, making their way now with no resistance. Beginning to move quickly through the prison, they called out the names of specific high profile leaders, releasing them first. These men were grouped together and moved down towards the beach. Big cheers went up from the prison's inhabitants, repeating in Arabic the chant of the Islamic extremists, "God is great! God is great! God is great!"

The small group of about one hundred select leaders detached from the rejoicing mob and sped down the beach, and into the boats that began to make their way through the slight chop of the surf to one of the waiting trawlers. Once alongside, they quickly scrambled up the side. They moved further along the deck and were greeted by those who made up the balance of the extremist league command group in the UK.

These were the men who had been the masterminds behind the infiltration; these were the higher-ups. These were the leaders, save for a few who had avoided capture, whose release had been the priority of the Islamic extremists. To ensure their safety was paramount.

As the first wave of newly released prisoners began to make their way as one solid group down to the beach, more began to pour out of the prison behind them, all shouting, 'God is great! God is great!' in Arabic.

As the first wave reached the ten RIB boats that were waiting to ferry them across to the freighters, the island was rocked by a series of blasts, almost like explosives were going off in different parts of the island. All the leaders' heads swung round and looked towards the prison, where so many thousands still worked their way towards the beach. With a loud clap, almost like the sound of thunder on judgement day, McRae Island turned into a blazing inferno as massive explosion upon massive explosion ripped through the prison and island, consuming everything as It expanded from its epicentre, and engulfing those who were standing on the beach in a wave of flame.

The force and sound of the percussion literally created shockwaves so strong that the trawlers down in the bay rocked on their anchors, causing those on the deck to be knocked off their feet. As they clambered back up, they turned in absolute horror and shock towards the island. The island had been filled with their key troops – the men and women in whom they had invested years of training and finance, their key assets in reaching every spectrum and level of society. Their elite Islamic Radical Extremist force had now, before their eyes, been eradicated in the fiery furnace that the island had become.

Over the noise of the screams and shouts of those dying on the island and the continuing explosions still rippling through the area, came the sound of helicopters. Out of the darkness they appeared, and from the night sky men and women in black overalls exploded out of the hovering helicopters, rappelling down the ropes onto the four freighters. Within minutes, there was a fierce firefight taking place on the decks. Gunfire sounded as men and women wearing night vision goggles swept through the freighters.

The firefight lasted for just fifteen minutes, but in the end all four freighters were under the control of the SAS and SAF Angel Group. However, in the chaos of the firefight, no one had seen the figure that had dived overboard into the cold waters.

Ishmael had made his break for freedom and had gone undetected.

CHAPTER ELEVEN

As the sun broke over McRae Island the morning after the firefight, elements of the Special Assault Force and the Special Air Services made their way across the burnt landscape. All around them there were many bodies to be seen, lifeless bodies burnt by the fireball that had exploded from within the island.

Rob looked across the devastation. "Stuart, what caused the explosions?" he asked.

Stuart looked at Rob and said, "I can't answer that now, but Bugs did tell me that these islands also stored a reserve of fuel. It is possible that there was a build-up of gas, or perhaps some stray shots hit one of the reservoirs setting off the chain reaction of explosions. I really cannot give a definitive answer. But one thing I know for sure, it was a very fortunate break for us, because it did take care of a large number of hostile people whom we would have spent years and years having to deal with through courts and interrogation. And in the long run, it would have cost the country millions."

Rob looked speculatively across at Stuart, trying to read his mind, looking deeply into his eyes. Was what happened here last night really an accident? Or could it have been a plan that this man, who had such a phenomenal military brain, was able to strategize? Did he know that this would be the result? Did he plant incendiary devices that caused the explosions? Had this been part of his master plan the whole way along? Rob was just not sure, and he would never know.

Stuart turned to Rob and said, "One thing that I did know for sure was that when the rescue attempt came, they would first of all identify their key players. It made sense that they would seek to get the command structure onto the trawlers as quickly as possible. I had planned for us to have our assault helicopters ready to deal with that. It was our plan to come in and take the trawlers under the cover of darkness once they had that first command group on board, and then move them out of the harbour leaving the rest of the prisoners stranded. What happened here... well, one day God will be the judge of exactly what took place."

"Well, Stuart," said Rob, "we can't dwell on what happened here, except to note as you said that it has dealt with more than eight thousand very militant fighters whose sole desire was to bring about the downfall of the United Kingdom. It's almost as if God did us a favour last night."

~~~~~

SAF Base, Cornwall

In the interrogation rooms, the different interrogation teams were working busily, seeking to extract information from the command group that they had brought in. It was proving to be a
~~~~~

challenging time, because these were the hard-core militants, the leaders of the lot. The interrogation of this group of men was not going to be easy. But Stuart knew that if they were going to make further inroads against this particular threat to the nation, they needed the intel that these men had.

As Stuart sat behind his desk, there was a knock at the door. "Enter," he called.

In came his son, Tom. Tom had been at the forefront of many of the sweeps across the country with his company, Angels 1. Lines of fatigue were written deeply into his face; the challenges that they had faced, the particular situations that they had had to deal with, had all left their toll on him and his men and women. He walked towards Stuart's desk and asked, "Permission to sit, Sir?"

"Of course," said his dad. "Take the weight off your feet."

Tom dropped wearily into a chair saying, "Well, Dad, we have been able to pull in a really good number. Our challenge now is going to be how to get the intel out of them."

Tom paused briefly before continuing, "One thing of interest that we did pick up is that one of the men who had made it to the boat with the command group wasn't there when we took them into custody. He was the Imam from the Sono Mosque in downtown London; his name is Ishmael. Somehow or other it seems that he got away, and that may be a challenge because from what we can establish so far, he is a key player. He was the one who radicalised and controlled the SAS group that turned traitor, so he is definitely a key figure in their operation.

"*I've* got a hunch this time, Dad; I'm sure we will see more of him in the future. I think he is somebody who carries a radical hatred for the United Kingdom – and in fact anything from the Western countries."

Stuart nodded his head. The news concerned him greatly; that the man who had been one of the key planners and leaders had somehow, despite all the best efforts of his team, managed to escape was a real disappointment.

"There is some good news, too," said Tom. "News is coming in from the United States and some of the countries in Europe; they have begun their own sweeps looking for people carrying the same spider and fist tattoo. To date, they have been able to identify significant numbers of them; and just like in our situation, they had infiltrated into just about every strata of society, every security force... just about everywhere."

"What is really concerning is that a high number of them were sitting at the European Court of Human Rights. Many of them were key planners, which would explain to a certain extent how some of the laws that have been put into place have made it so difficult for us to be able to deal with the radicals that have been in the country. By appealing to the Charter of Human Rights and to the Court of Human Rights, they have been able to get away with staying in the country – all the while continuing to radicalise young people – instead of being deported back to the countries that they came from."

"It is good news that we've been able to identify them now," said Stuart. He sat thoughtfully, pondering the new intel before continuing, "But there is another area that does concern me, and that's the number of refugee ships that are constantly being allowed to gain entry to the different countries in Europe. This is something we really need to deal with.

"Bugs has been looking at the different demographics of those on the ships; 98% of them are males, almost all of them aged between 20 and 35. I've got a funny feeling that many of these 'refugees' are actually trained Jihadi warriors using the guise of coming in as refugees to get a foothold here. That's something we will have to deal with in the future, something that must be discussed with Mr Cribbs and Cobra next time we have a meeting with them."

Tom leaned back in his chair and said, "Dad, there is something else that's been on my mind. As a unit we have been getting a huge amount of publicity, and as such it is now common knowledge that we are based here in Cornwall. We all have families with children, and I think we need to look at stepping up the security around our base; we have just become prime target number one for just about every radical in the Islamic world. We need to be really careful and take special care with our own security."

"I agree with you 100%," said Stuart. "As a matter of fact, I am already putting together a number of proposals and policies that we will discuss at command group. I am also pulling together a special unit from within the Angels. The new unit's sole task will be to focus on the families of those who are serving within this unit and keep them safe. We also want to make sure that extended families are also watched over and kept secure."

Stuart leaned forward, steepling his fingers as he continued, "I've got a meeting tomorrow with Mr Cribbs and Cobra. I will be putting a number of proposals on the table. In addition to what we've already discussed, the intel coming through has highlighted some more very alarming matters. One that most concerns me is the fact that the radical Islamic Jihadists have training camps in strategic countries all over the world. And you may be sad to hear this, Tom, but the intel that we have received so far suggests there are camps in South Africa, Zimbabwe and Zambia.

"It seems that these three southern African countries that we know well have been helping the Jihadi warriors. There is further intel to suggest that this is happening in other parts of the world as well. I will be speaking to Mr Cribbs about changing our brief; we need to be able to have the capacity to deal not only with the threat within our own borders, but we also need the authority and the equipment to be able to go beyond our borders – to strike at these Jihadi warriors in their places of training, to strike at the countries and the leaders of the countries that are supporting them. We've all seen that diplomacy doesn't work, because the politicians will agree with you on one hand, but with the other they are supporting and helping these Jihadi warriors within their own country. The threat that is arising through all the different militant groups working or joining together is something that we are going to have to deal with."

Stuart took a deep breath and looking Tom in the eye, he continued, "That means, Son, that we will soon have to look at expanding the size of the unit; we will need more men and women, and they will have to be committed Christians. They will have to be men and women who are available to God, men and women trained to the highest level, if we are to deal with this continuing threat."

"I agree with you wholeheartedly, Dad," said Tom. "I can't wait until we can really get stuck in and deal with this threat and give It such a blow that it will never ever be able to rise again."

Stuart rocked back in his chair. "Well, Son, I think we've delivered a massive blow to them here in the United Kingdom; I think we've literally ripped the heart out of their operation. It may be years before they will be in a position to once again mount the sort of assault that they were planning. However, I think the other countries of Europe, and perhaps even in the United States, will face far greater challenges. Because we stumbled onto this, we were able to deal with it quickly and decisively; however, the radicals in their own countries have had more time to evade capture, and it will be more and more difficult to deal with them. They will face real challenges, and I think ultimately we will need a multinational cooperating force.

"That said, I can assure you of one thing: we as the Angels will only effectively allow into our unit, men and women who have a saving knowledge of God, men and women who know Jesus Christ as their own Lord and Saviour."

Tom nodded his head in agreement. "You're right, Dad. The truth is that we wrestle here not against flesh and blood, but against principalities and powers and a spiritual force of wickedness that is almost frightening in its intensity."

"Absolutely, Tom," Stuart agreed.

Tom then smiled and with a twinkle in his eye asked his dad, "So what are we going to do with the Countess of St Ives?" He was referring of course to his sister, Storm.

Stuart smiled at the thought of his daughter, "We will be bringing her on board as a logistics officer; I need somebody like her to be working alongside Bugs. Her ability to analyse all the different things that are going down, plus her other unique skills, will be an asset. Storm's diagnostic skills are legendary, and her ability to pull a lot of information together accurately and with insight is going to be vital to this unit. I haven't spoken to her yet, but I think she will come on board. That's the plan."

Tom looked across at his dad. "And Steve?"

"Well, Steve came to speak with me; he would love to try out for selection and be given an opportunity to join this unit. That is really something that Steve and Storm need to chat through, but I would love to give him the opportunity, because I believe that he would be an asset to the unit," said Stuart.

Stuart rose from his chair, walked across to Tom and placed his hand on his son's shoulder giving it a big squeeze, "Tom, I am proud of you. You have been through a lot in a very short time, but I'm just so proud to see how you've grown, how you lead your men, the rapport that you've developed with them. And I really love their nickname for you. I think it will become your permanent call sign, 'Lord Dude'... No, wait; maybe it should just be 'Dude'; we don't want you getting a big head. Yes, I think we'll just use 'Dude'; that's an easy way for us to identify you."

Tom came to his feet, and reached across and gave his dad a hug saying, "Dad, thank you. I appreciate all the opportunities that you have given me and the example that you have been."

Tom straightened up, a smile coming to his face as the direction of his thoughts changed. "We are all eating at your house tonight; rumour has it that Mom is making one of those fantastic roasts, and you know how much we all love her cooking!"

Stuart looked across at his son with affection. "Absolutely right! Let's forget about all this security stuff, and let's walk across to the house and go and have a really good old-fashioned roast meal. And I think I'll put away my Beret and the accoutrements of war and just spend the next few hours being a granddad, kidding around and wrestling with my grandchildren."

Tom gave a laugh and said, "Love that command." And together they exited the room.

~~~~~

The fisherman had been out early. He knew some of the best fishing spots around McRae Island in the Outer Hebrides. Cutting through the water with his little boat, he saw what first appeared to be a bundle of seaweed floating close inshore; but as he drew closer, he saw it was a man. Grabbing his boathook, he reached over and hooked at the man's clothes pulling him closer to the boat.

As he lifted the body into the boat, he saw it was an Arab man – an Arab man with a very dark complexion, a complexion that was showing a bluish tinge after being in the cold water exposed to the elements for so long. The fisherman quickly grabbed a pile of blankets from down below and piled them on top of the freezing man; he felt for and found a very faint pulse.

Fishing forgotten, he turned his boat around and headed for his hut on one of the nearby remote islands. Pulling into his little dock, the fisherman lifted the man – showing a strength that belied his age – and carried the stranger inside. He soon began
~~~~~

the process of gently warming the man up, gradually bringing him back up to full body temperature.

Over the next few days the fisherman slowly revived and treated the man that he had pulled from the sea, the Imam, Ishmael.

Slowly Ishmael regained his strength. A few days after the rescue, Ishmael, now nearly back at full strength, looked across at the old fishermen and asked, "So what are you going to do now?"

The fishermen quietly observed the stranger in his home. Eventually, he responded to the Imam's question, "Well, what I should do is report you to the authorities. However, I've lived my whole life on this island. I've been alone. I have no friends, I have no family, and I don't trust anybody in government or anybody in the establishment."

The old man paused a moment before continuing, "My opinion has always been that everybody should be free to go about their own business; so, when you're ready, I'll take you to the mainland, drop you off and you can do what you need to do. I don't know the full story of what's been going on in the UK, and I don't know the full story of what happened on McRae Island. Yes, I saw the fireball and the helicopters and all the military operations there, but as far as I'm concerned, you're free to do whatever you want.'"

Ishmael smiled. The Great One was smiling down on him. He had been found by probably one of the few people in the United Kingdom who was not prepared to turn him in, an old fisherman who in fact had never even asked his name.

A few days later the fisherman did exactly what he had said. The old man dropped Ishmael on the mainland with a change of clothes, and even gave him some money to see him on his way, not realising at the time that he was releasing one of the most dangerous men on earth back into society to begin to devise the plans that could bring the whole world into jeopardy.

The old fisherman climbed back in his boat and began to row away. Ishmael turned, gave one wave and then disappeared into the darkness to begin the long and arduous journey to Syria, to get to the place where he could begin to determine what was left of the shattered remnants of the fist.

There, he would begin to plan again, and this time they would plan more wisely than they had before. They would plan in such a way that they would be able to simultaneously bring a blow to all the nations of the Western world – a blow that would bring them to their knees. The Western World on its knees would be ripe for conquest and judgement.

The hatred that burned in him was like a corrosive acid burning through his soul; he just could not come to terms with the fact that the country that had taken him in, fed him and educated him, housed and treated him was anything other than a despotic Western country.

His mind had been so twisted and blinded by the radical teachings that he had received, that he had reached the point where he was no longer capable of rational thought. His radical thoughts had become his norm, his reality, and had robbed him of all mercy and sympathy. In fact, they had robbed him of almost all of the human characteristics and the nature he had once as a child possessed.

CHAPTER TWELVE

Number 10 Downing Street
Half an hour before the Cobra meeting

Stuart and Rob were sitting down across the table from Mr Cribbs, the Prime Minister.

"Sir," said Stuart, "I really think that we need to take some deep decisions here. Let me outline my concerns. The first is that we are about to go into the Cobra meeting – a meeting that includes a number of liberal politicians who are part of the coalition government. That to me is an immediate security risk."

David Cribbs looked across at Stuart and said, "What do you suggest?"

"David, I think you need to call for an amendment to the 'Fixed Term Parliament Act' to allow you to request an emergency general election. At the moment the nation is so shocked about what has happened, is so shocked at the level of penetration of the Islamic extremists, that your particular shares in terms of a politician are riding very high. The people respect the fact that you took decisive action, that you stepped into the gap and did what needed to be done even in the face of a lot of opposition and the fact that it could have destroyed your political career.

"Mr Prime Minister, you need a clear mandate from the people to be able to govern. We need a situation, where we can go to security meeting like Cobra and know that we do not have to deal with a large number of liberals – men who have aggressively pursued their own agenda and put in place a lot of the laws and policies that allowed these Islamic extremists to penetrate as deeply as they did into every strata of our society.

"Sir, here again I think you need to act decisively. I think we need a government that can govern without a coalition, and we need a Security Council that is *secure*. We need to be certain that we will not have people on board whose sympathies lie elsewhere and who may be a security risk. With that in mind, Sir, I have no intention of outlining all of our plans and policies today in this Cobra meeting. I believe the security risks are just too great with the liberal Deputy Prime Minister and other members of his party sitting on that board. I think we need, today, to stick to generalities, and then have a more private discussion about the more serious matters that we need to address."

David Cribbs looked across at Rob and Stuart and said, "Tell me about some of those things."

"First of all, we need to realise that we have significant issues arising out of the intel that is coming in," said Stuart. "We have a number of very hostile nations that on the face of it appear to be our friends, nations we are actually giving aid to, but who behind our backs are providing support, training facilities and logistical support to this Al Qaeda movement."

Stuart paused for a moment to allow the impact of his words to settle, before continuing, "David, I believe that the mandate for my unit needs to change; it needs to be expanded. I believe that, without sacrificing our core responsibility of securing the United Kingdom, we also need to be able to go forward and move beyond our borders to strike at those who pose a threat to our nation – in particular, we need to target the training camps and those politicians who are giving them the resources that they need. They need to understand that regardless of who they are, or where they are, we can reach them – and we will reach them!"

David Cribbs looked across at Stuart, "And you don't think we'll be able to do that through a process of diplomacy?"

"Mr Prime Minister, I believe that what we are dealing with is a hardened enemy, an enemy that will on one hand appear to be our friends but at the same time will be sharpening the knife to stick in our backs. We need to show them decisively that we will not be dictated to, that we will not allow them to continue to train within their borders the men and the women who will come back and be suicide bombers, come back and seek to infiltrate, come back and seek to break down all that we have done and sought to build," Stuart replied.

David looked really thoughtful. Finally, he said, "Very well, Stuart, I believe what you're saying is right."

At this juncture Rob jumped into the discussion and added, "Sir, I believe that both the SAS and the SAF need to become really dark units, keeping under the radar as much as possible. They need to have a combined commander who is able to deal with them, and perhaps one or two other units that we need to create or add to the team to be able deal with the specific logistical problems that are going to arise."

David Cribbs looked across at Rob and said, "Your proposals, General."

"Well, Sir, I propose that we allow Stuart to take supreme command of those two units and also give him the authority to be able to call on any other unit within the United Kingdom, so that he can do what needs to get done without getting bogged down by all the backroom politics that may come his way. I propose bringing back the rank of Field Marshall and promoting Stuart to that rank. That way there will be no question as to who outranks whom, and we will be able to cut through much of the inter-force politics."

Mr Cribbs looked across at Rob and clarified, "So what we are talking about then is somebody like Monty or Eisenhower, somebody who has the authority to do what needs to get done and is answerable only to me?"

"Absolutely, Mr Prime Minister," Rob replied, "You've hit it on the head."

"Well, that is a road I think we can go down," replied David Cribbs.

Stuart now chipped in and said, "Mr Prime Minister, we also need to lift martial law. But I think in light of everything that's happened that we need to maintain a state of emergency for the next twelve months, running up to a new election period. This will give us the extraordinary powers that we may need to go in and do what we need to do."

David Cribbs nodded his head. "I concur," he said. "I think the next twelve months are going to be critical, not only for us as a nation but for America as well. Okay, gentlemen, thank you for sharing your concerns with me before the meeting; it is time for us to be going. We have some things to put on the table before Cobra, but as you said, let's keep to generalities rather than specifics; we don't want a security breach to happen from within our own Cobra meeting."

Together, the men moved across to the door and entered into a much larger room where the different members of the Cobra committee were sitting. David Cribbs introduced Stuart – Rob was well known to them already – and they sat down and began to discuss the particular issues that were arising.

Mr Cribbs looked to the intelligence officer who had come along to brief them and said, "Okay, John, let's hear it."

John stood up and, with quite a sombre voice due to the gravity of the situation, began to outline the reports coming in from the neighbouring nations as well as those from the United States.

"The USA has a massive problem. Their sweeps have not picked up 8,000 like ours did; they figure at this stage they are sitting closer to 15,000. And they have found these Islamic moles in just about every single level. The intensity with which they have been able to get into every single level of society is frightening. The same reports are coming through from the nations of Europe. We are dealing with a mess of massive proportions. "

Stuart turned round and began to address the Cobra members, "Gentlemen, there are a number of other issues that we need to address. One of the things I would like to put on the table is the freedom with which these so-called refugee boats are gaining entrance into Europe. Look at the demographics of the people on them; 98% of them fit the profile of the Jihadi warrior. That needs to be stopped, even if it means taking a hard-core line. I think that we need to turn them around and escort them back to where they came from and not allow them to set foot in Europe. If that doesn't work, then we need to make it very clear that we would regard any of those boats coming our way as an invasion, and we would sink the ship or ships."

The Deputy Prime Minister jumped up, a look of absolute horror and anger on his face, "You can't do that! It goes against the Bill of Human Rights."

Stuart turned and looked him in the eye, "With all due respect, Mr Deputy Prime Minister, it is your championing of all these different laws of human rights that have given the necessary means to the extremists and criminals to allow them a 'get out of jail free' card. This bill has allowed them to do the things that they do with the level of impunity they have employed. YOU, Sir, and others like you have been responsible for the systematic dismantling of our systems of defence; you've turned our borders into porous walls where people can almost pass through at will; you've shackled our armed forces and our police forces; you've taken over courts and you've limited them; and you've given power to somebody outside of our borders to determine what is right or wrong."

The Deputy Prime Minister's face turned bright red. He was clearly preparing to blast out again with all his liberal ideologies.

Stuart leaned forward and with steel in his voice said, "With all due respect, Sir, let me tell you categorically that I have no respect for you or any of your mates. You live in your privileged dream world, far removed from reality. I challenge you to test just how open the world is to all your liberal human rights without some form of balance. You, Sir, need to go and walk through the streets of Syria, Afghanistan, Iraq and Libya. Walk through them unarmed and unescorted. Walk through them and see how long you will survive. I can guarantee it won't be very long before you are lying dead in the desert sand, your head lopped off."

The Deputy Prime Minister reared back in shock – first of all at the fact that somebody would take him on, and second, that a direct challenge had been brought to him.

Stuart was relentless; he followed up his first barrage with a second. "Sir, the day that you are prepared to do that will be the day that I will be prepared to respect you and the members of your party. *But until then* you will not have my respect, nor the respect of any of my men.

"Let me tell you a home truth; you don't have the respect of the Armed Forces of this country, and you don't have the respect of the police force. In fact if you look at your opinion polls, you are sitting here just because a small portion of the population voted for you. And that allowed you to be a kingpin. But let me tell you: your days are numbered, because if we hadn't come across this particular plot when we did, the Islamic flag would have been flying over London before too long."

That long overdue dose of truth firmly delivered by Stuart had the deputy prime minister sinking back in his chair, too shocked to speak, but also beginning to come to terms with the reality of the fact that the population of Britain – and especially the Armed Forces – had absolutely no respect for him or his ilk, and that they were prepared to stand up and take him on.

Stuart turned to face the other members of Cobra committee, "Ladies and gentlemen, we also need to face the fact that there are huge swathes of our countryside, huge swathes of our property right here in London, that belong to people who have very strong sympathies with the radical Islamic warriors whom we have been fighting."

David Cribbs turned to Stuart and asked the question, "What do you suggest?"

"That we suspend all foreign ownership of property by all who might have Islamic militant sympathies, that is by people who have come out of or still reside in Islamic countries. They have bought huge swathes of London, and they need to be subject to a full investigation into where the money to purchase their properties originated and where their sympathies lie. Also, the security force must have the freedom to move in and out of these properties at will to check them and prevent them from becoming havens, where the radical Islamic Jihadi warriors can gather, train and brainwash the vulnerable youth of today."

Stuart outlined all the policies and recommendations that he had put forward, and then he and Rob excused themselves from the Cobra meeting and made their way outside to the car that was waiting to whisk them across to the helicopter that would airlift them to their respective bases.

~~~~~

Three hours later Stuart was back at the SAF base in Cornwall when his phone rang. Lifting the receiver, he heard the Prime Minister, David Cribbs, at the other end.
~~~~~

"All our recommendations were unanimously carried at the Cobra meeting. The Deputy Prime Minister excused himself soon after you left," chuckled David. "You really gave him a rocket. Now, you've been promoted to Field Marshal with immediate effect, and you've been given supreme control over the Armed Forces of the United Kingdom, specifically the SAS, your own Special Assault Force and any other units you choose to add to that unique group.

"There is something else that affects you, and this was decided in a closed much smaller Cobra meeting, so we could be absolutely sure that there was no security breach; we've given you the authority to run both internal and external operations.

"I'll be announcing this evening that we will be lifting martial law, but that we will be putting in its place a state of emergency. Also, in light of the threat that has come against us as a nation, we will be calling for an early general election within the next two months so that we can get a clear mandate from the people whether they want us to govern; or whether they're happy to go along with the hodgepodge coalition of people, who ultimately in their core ideology, are an absolute threat to the things we need to do in order to secure our nation."

Stuart replied with relief, "'Mr Prime Minister, I'm absolutely pleased to hear that; it's good news. I'll get the wheels in motion and will begin to move on the intel that we have already. Thank you so much, Mr Prime Minister. Thank you for having the courage to do what you needed to do when it needed to be done; you have our respect. Thank you and good night. Have a good evening."

Stuart walked across his office, popped his head through into the operations room and said, "Right, please request all Angels commanders to join me. And please get onto the SAS; ask Rob and Joe if they will also be available for a quick conference call. We need to start moving on some new developments as soon as we can."

~~~~~

Stuart looked at the Angels' commanders who were now gathered around the operations table, and he began to brief them on all the changes that would be taking place. There was very animated discussion in terms of the fact that they would now have to expand the unit size, as well as develop an internal unit within the unit for the protection of the unit personnel. The discussions grew more lively as they sat around and looked at the different options and the various things that they would need to do, all of this linked together with the possibility of external ops to other countries.

In the middle of their discussions, Bugs popped his head around the door and said, "Hulk, you had better come quickly; there has been a major incident at Heathrow."
Stuart and all the other commanders leapt up from the table and quickly made their way to the Ops
~~~~~

room. There on the big screen, TV stations were showing the wreckage of an airliner that had come down in a field not far from Heathrow. At first indications it would appear, according to eyewitnesses, that what looked to be a missile was seen streaking through the air and hitting the plane, thus bringing it down.

Just then the on-site reporter for BBC news came online and said, "Yes, we can confirm that on board the stricken jet was Vince Cobble, one of the MPs for Parliament and the Cabinet's Business Secretary."

Tom thinking out loud voiced the question, "Could it be possible that this plane was deliberately targeted due to the high value passenger?"

Stuart's mind began to race. Heathrow was one of the busiest airports in the world, with hundreds of flights coming in to land every day – somewhere in the region of one every sixty seconds. For a surface to air missile to have hit a specific plane, the attacker must have had very specific data, not to mention the equipment to dial that data into. Stuart thought for a moment, then turned to Tom and the other commanders and said, "Isn't there an app that people can get on their iPads and iPhones called Flighttracker 24? An app that allows you to accurately pinpoint a plane? I believe you can identify the plane's flight number, its altitude and speed."
Bugs nodded his head, "Absolutely! That is available and very popular."

"Well," said Stuart, "I think there is a strong probability that what we're dealing with here is somebody who has got hold of a missile launcher; there are a number of them available. Somebody could have used that app and literally identified the flight, put the data into the launcher and fired the missile. What we are dealing with here is definitely a terrorist attack."

Stuart then turned to Bugs and said, "Bugs, I want to get the Air Force on the line. Tell them I want us to have a squadron of six jets over Heathrow, six over Gatwick and another six over Stansted. We will also have to put two or three over every single major airport in the UK. Tell them I want them all equipped with anti-missile technology. They can deploy chaff between the missile and its target if needs be, and in the worst case scenario, take the hit themselves to save the airliner. They need to be patrolling just in case another strike is launched, in which case they will need to sweep in and get between the missile and the airliner to release their anti-missile measures.

"I am pretty certain this is a strike that is payback by some of the Jihadists, *but* the key question in my mind is how on earth these people knew that somebody like Vince Cobble was going to be on board. How did they know to target that specific flight? It means they must have had access to the passenger list, so I think we have to move the operation to London.

"Tom, I need you to get your section. Go to Heathrow and check everybody who had access to that information. The rest of you, we are going to do another sweep. Let's check the personnel, check their backgrounds; all aspects need to be covered. Remember that some of them may have had the tattoo, but may have had it removed by laser. There will always be a sign, some scarring, even if it has been removed. Let's check it out quickly; we need to get on top of this. Also, we'll need to bring the SAS in to help. Bugs, can you get them on the phone for me?"

Stuart got back into his own office just as the phone rang. As Bugs made the connection, he picked it up and said,

"Hi, Joe. I know you will be up to speed on this incident that has gone down at Heathrow; BBC suggests that they're talking about 300 to 320 casualties. It appears that after the missile strike, the pilot was able to direct the plane to an open area; if it had come down in a highly populated area, we would be looking at a higher number of casualties.

"Joe, we have to get resources on the ground. To begin with we have to put up snipers on highpoints around all of the flight paths. I think the maximum launch range for some of these particular missiles is within one or two miles, so we need to have a ring of sniper and spotter teams set up all around. This missile could be launched from anyone's back garden. I don't think it will be the only one; I think they will be giving it another shot. Let's have a team scanning all the CCTV cameras in case they can pick up anything; and let's get our computer buffs working out, more or less, based on the trajectory, where this particular rocket was launched from."

Stuart continued, "I'll be on my way up to London now together with the teams; you can contribute your teams as well. We will need assault teams and every sniper team that you have available."

Joe on the other end of the line said, "Roger that, Stuart. We're good to go."

Three hours later the teams were on-site in London. They began to set up and moved around the crash site, working out the possible trajectories of the missile that had brought down the airliner. The radio crackled into life, "Hulk, Hulk, do you copy?"

"Roger, Dude, this is Hulk. Go," said Stuart.

"Roger, Hulk. We've gone through the personnel and identified three that are possible hostiles."

"Right," said Stuart, "we need to move on that now. Do we have addresses? Are any of them at work?"

Tom came back and said, "Negative. None of them are at work, but we have eyes on their homes."

"Roger that, Dude. Let's start rolling on that; if you can send me the addresses, I'll get our teams moving," confirmed Stuart.

Half an hour later the teams were overhead. Helicopters were the operational standard, quick to move through London, especially with the heavy traffic that London experiences. Stuart himself was part of one assault team; he turned to his guys in the helicopter, and made contact with the units at the other two addresses and said, "Right, guys. On my go, we rappel down and we hit the house – one team from the back, one from the front. Angels 2, Angels 3, do you copy?"

The radio came back to life. "Roger that. Copy. We are good to go," came the response from the other two locations.

"Roger, then this is a go. Green, green. Go, go," yelled Stuart.

Within seconds the men and women were rappelling down the ropes and landing in the streets, moving swiftly up to the front and back doors of the identified properties. Entry was made very swiftly and professionally as they moved their way through the doors, some members peeling off to deal with the ground floor, the others moving up the stairs to the floors above. Stuart, leading his team up to the first floor, saw a hostile armed with an AK-47 appear on the landing. Instincts took over. There was a pop, pop from Stuart's HK416-D10RS rifle, and the person tumbled down the stairs.
The unit swept upwards. All through the house came the sounds of intermittent gunfire, as they engaged the extremists being harboured there.

Within fifteen minutes the Special Force unit had contained the whole area. Stuart began to get the report back coming over the radio from his men.

Angels 2 reported in, ""Roger. At our location we encountered armed resistance. I can confirm the death of five, I say again, five hostiles in total. One of our men was hit as well; he is being casevaced out to the hospital now, but it is going to be touch and go."

Stuart's heart turned very heavy. This was the first casualty that they had experienced as a unit, and it really wasn't a good feeling.

"Roger that, Angels 2. Please confirm which hospital the casualty has been taken to," requested Stuart.

"Roger, Hulk. The Royal London Hospital, one of the very best," replied the Angels 2 commander.

"Roger that, Angels 2. Well done to all involved."

Intel began to pour in; they had indeed uncovered three more Al Qaeda nests with Jihadi Warriors, both men and women, all of them home-grown and native to the United Kingdom. Of the three that worked at Heathrow, two were among the dead; but they had been able to capture the third one alive. They would start very intensive interrogation of that particular person to try and identify the others, and in particular the details and number of missile launchers involved.

What did come out was that there was evidence that these particular groups were armed with rocket launchers; they also found on one laptop computer the itinerary of all flights in and out of Manchester airport. Stuart found this very interesting.

"Okay, let's make sure we've got teams on the ground in Manchester. I'm going over to the hospital now," Stuart said to his 2IC.

~~~~~

A short time later, Stuart arrived at the hospital and made his way through the doors. The Angels 2 commander was already there. He came up to Stuart and said, "They've just taken Corporal Cook through to surgery."

"Okay. Give me the details," said Stuart.

"We made entry and started to move up. Team 1 was in the lead with Corporal Cook in front, and this Jihadi chap was literally lying at the top of the stairs with his AK-47; he put a full mag on auto in Cookie's direction. Corporal Cook caught the blast head on; his body armour took some of the hits, but unfortunately it looks like two rounds hit his neck. Another round seems to have slipped in between his helmet and his goggles, and we're not quite sure what damage has been done. But it didn't look good... doesn't sound good," said the Angels 2 Commander, a Captain Trevor Sparks.

Stuart and Trevor found some chairs on the landing. As they sat, Stuart prayed quietly. "Lord, You know this is Your situation. You know Corporal Cook knows You as Lord; You also know that he's got a young wife and that she is expecting a baby. I do bring him before you, Lord; his injuries are horrendous, but we just trust You to do what You
~~~~~

need to do in this situation. Lord, we trust You for the outcome whatever it is".

For the next half hour Stuart and the Angels 2 commander walked up and down; they just didn't seem to be able to rest. And then the doors swung open. And the surgeon moved towards them. They could see from the look on his face that it wasn't good news.

"Gentlemen, I am sorry. We did everything we could, but unfortunately the two shots in the neck created serious damage. We may have been able to repair that; however, the round that hit him in the head lodged in his brain and appeared to have caused irreparable damage. While we were trying to do what we could on the operating table, he suffered cardiac arrest and we lost him."

Stuart could feel tears welling up in his eyes at the passing of this brave young man. Images flashed across his mind: the young man on selection, the pride he took in leading his section of men, his young wife and the joy that they had expressed when they had heard the news that they were going to be a mom and dad. Stuart felt the anger well up in him at these Jihadi extremists who saw nothing wrong with just going out and bringing down the innocent. Stuart thought of the hundreds of people who had just this very day died in the airliner; and once again he could feel that deep anger – that desire to eradicate this evil from the face of the earth – welling up within him.

He turned round and said, "Thanks, Doc. We appreciate all that you did."

Stuart got back up on the radio and said, "This is an all net broadcast, all net broadcast. Angels, I am really sorry to tell you that we lost Cooksey today. I'm on a flight back to Cornwall, so that I can be the one to tell his wife."

Right across the radio net the calls came in — calls of sorrow and of anger as the different units acknowledged the broadcast. Stuart came back up on the radio net and said, "Dude, Dude, do you copy?"

"Roger, Hulk, reading you fives." Heaviness was clearly evident in Tom's voice."

"Dude," said Stuart, "I need you to take command. I'm flying back to Cornwall to break the news to Cooksey's wife. With the intel we have, we can be prepared. I've got a funny feeling that these guys will seek to strike again very soon. Make sure we have all the passenger portfolios of all the flights going in or out. I want our guys scanning them to see if there are any high-profile targets emerging."

"Roger that, Sir," said Dude. "Please give our condolences to Corporal Cook's wife. Dude out."

~~~~~~

Three hours later Stuart made his way, together with Jane, up towards the doorway of the little bungalow that Corporal Cook and his wife called home. Stuart knocked on the door and Bev answered, a bouncy,
~~~~~~

beautiful 24 year old so full of life. She was glowing with the new life that was growing within her.

"Hi, Stuart and Jane, good to see you," greeted Bev. And then she stopped mid-sentence as she realised that Stuart was still dressed in his combat gear and she noticed the grief and the pain etched on his face. She went pale and started to sag at the knees in shock. Jane moved forward and grabbed her in support. Stuart put his arms around them both.

"Bev," he said, "I'm just so sorry; we lost Chris today. He was leading his section up the stairs, and there was a contact with Jihadi extremists. Unfortunately, he was shot multiple times, and three of the shots were in areas that his body armour couldn't protect. Chris was shot twice in the throat and once in the head; the doctors did all they could to save him."

As Stuart was saying these words, tears began to roll down his face – and down Jane's face as well. "I'm just so sorry," he said.

They stood there for a while, just attempting to control the pain and the agony that they were feeling. Then Bev broke the moment by taking a step back and saying, "It's okay, Stuart. Chris knew the Lord; and while the pain that I am experiencing now is unbelievable, I know that Chris is seated at the right hand of the King of Kings and Lord of Lords. Right now he is sitting down at the banqueting table of the King, and I know that's my final destination one day, too. My job now – and for the future – is to make sure that our unborn child, the child that is the fruit of Chris' and my love and of our commitment to each other and to the Lord, is brought safely into the world. And that she gets to know what a hero her dad was.

Bev covered her face as the tears really started to pour down her cheeks. Jane came close again, gathered Bev into her arms and just held her. Stuart came up and put his arm around them as well and said, "Don't worry, Bev. We will see to it that you are taken care of. I promise that you and your unborn child will not want for anything. Our guys will be taking care of you; you will be looked after, and there will be a home for you within this unit for as long as you need it."

Stuart then started to pray and said, "Lord, I commit Bev and her unborn child to you. Lord, I pray that in the days, weeks, months and years ahead that You would be their shield and sufficiency. Thank You that this is not goodbye, that one day we will be reunited with Chris as we stand in that multitude that will stand around Your throne. Thank You, Jesus, that death does not have dominion over us, and we can know the reality of that promise and eternal security in Jesus Christ. Thank You, Lord; we love You."

Jane had put out the call to some of the other young wives; and as Stuart and Jane were about to leave the little bungalow' some of them were making their way up. They knew that Bev would be okay, that her sisters in Christ would gather around and watch over and support her.

As Stuart and Jane made their way down the road past the NCO's staff quarters, Stuart turned to Jane and said, "Love, thank you so much for being there to help me with that."

Jane reached for her husband of so many years and just gave him a hug. "Stuart, I know how much this is hurting you. You take every single one of these young men and women in your command into your heart, and I know how difficult it is and the weight of responsibility that you feel. Stuart, I want you to know that God will be your strength, your shield; and as we prayed, we believe we have that wonderful promise that God is in control!"

Jane continued, "Every time you and Tom go out my heart aches, and I pray for you all so much. But I know you must do what God has called you to do in relation to this evil that is seeking to destroy and break down. I want you to know, Stuart, that I love you, and I am here for you."

Stuart reached down and gathered his wife into his arms. "Jane, you are so precious. I am just so blessed that God brought you into my life. Honey, thank you. Please continue to pray for us; we've got some really challenging things to do and deal with, and we need all the prayer that we can get. I need to be off to London as soon as I've had a quick word with Bugs. I need to be back up there with my team."

Jane looked across at her husband, then put her arms up around his neck and pulled him down, giving him a deep, comforting kiss.

"Stuart, you do what you have to do. Know that I'll be upholding you and the team in prayer and taking care of Bev," reassured Jane.

~~~~~

Four hours later Stuart was back in London. The cold was settling and seeping in; he gave a shiver – from the cold, yes, but also from the sense of evil that he could feel prowling around, just like the Word of God says. *The enemy, the devil, prowls around like a roaring lion seeking someone to devour.* And that's exactly what Stuart was feeling – that the enemy was on the prowl seeking someone to devour.

As he moved into the makeshift command post that they had set up close to Heathrow airport, he sent up a silent prayer. "Lord Jesus, give me the wisdom and insight to be able to find out where these people are; I just pray that you would help us."

Stepping into the tent, Stuart made his way across to his intelligence team and said, "Right, guys, what can you give me?"

"Well, Hulk," said his intelligence officer, "we've got pretty solid intel from the info that we found on the laptop and from the interrogations that we've done so far. It would appear that there are three teams operating, three ground to air launchers. We have also established that they have two men
~~~~~

per team, so we've got six people out there. Intel seems to indicate that one of them moved up to Manchester; the other two were operating in London, one around Heathrow and one around Gatwick."

"Roger that," said Stuart. "What else?"

"Well, Sir, there is a flight going out at 11:15pm this evening that's carrying some very high-profile Jordanian ministers," reported his intel officer.

"Right, that would be a target – especially for the Islamic extremists, because they see Jordan as an ally of the West in some instances. Okay, get me the Air Force on the line."

Within a few seconds Stuart was talking with the Air Force over the radio. "Right, guys, we really need to keep this jet coverage in place and very tight. It's almost impossible for us to identify where the extremists will fire from, but we have got teams up in high places. Our sniper teams have infrared technology in place, and we have some satellite surveillance. I really need your boys to look sharp if these guys launch another missile. They need to be able to get between the missile and its target and deploy the anti-missile resources."

The voice that came back over the radio was confident saying, "No problem, Sir. Our boys will be able to do that; they are the best in the world."

"Roger. Tell them to be on their toes; we've got a possibility that just may develop after 23:00 hours.

Please make sure you have six jets in the air and overhead."

Just then Stuart's intelligence officer came across to him and said, "Sir, we've got some more intel. We have a flight leaving out of Gatwick within five minutes of the flight at Heathrow, and the plane is carrying a number of Saudi ministers together with the UK trade delegation making their way out to Saudi for further discussions."

"They would be another high-profile target," confirmed Stuart. He immediately got back onto the Air Force and said, "Can you blue jobs also cover Gatwick? We just received further intel that the Jihadists could be after a high-profile target there as well?"

"Roger that. We have six jets over Gatwick, and they will remain in place," replied the Air Force Liaison Officer.

"Roger," said Stuart. "And thanks to you guys in the blue jobs; we appreciate you." Breaking off the connection, Stuart came back up on his own battle net and called to all his different units.

"We've got two possibilities — one at Heathrow and one at Gatwick. All sniper teams, I want you to be wide awake. Same goes for the observation teams; I want your infrared technology working the moment the missile launches. We will acquire an initial heat signature at the point of launch; I want you to lock down that position faster than ants at a picnic. Once pinpointed, all snipers, your guns are hot; if you can get a shot, take it. Just make sure you've got a positive identification; I don't want you taking out some dad setting off fireworks. If you can see the guys, take them down."

"Roger that, Hulk," was the call back from all the units.

Stuart made his way over to the coffee maker. After making himself a cup of coffee, he sat quietly sipping it and feeling it ease the cold. His intel officer came and joined him, asking the question, "Are you okay, Hulk?"

"I'm fine. Thanks," he said. "I just hate sitting around having to wait; I'm more of a front-line man myself. I like to be in the very thick of the action."

The intel officer smiled; he had seen the Hulk in action and knew that to be true. "Sir, sometimes God just needs you to sit and listen, to use the wisdom and the insight that He has given you to help all of us to be able to do what we need to do. You've put a solid plan in place; we just have to wait," observed the intel officer.

As the clock ticked over towards 23:00 hours, Stuart could feel the tension rising. He could feel the adrenaline starting to pump, feel the alertness coming back into his body and his mind as his vision cleared and everything became brighter. At 23:05 the radio crackled into life.

"Roger, Roger, the BA flight has just taken off; it's starting to climb," reported one observation group.
"Okay, boys and girls," Stuart said, "heads up! It could be party time."

Three minutes later the radio came alive. "Hulk, we have a launch; we have a launch," reported one of the sniper teams.

"Confirm, confirm, we have a launch. Do you have a visual on the launchers confirmed?" queried Stuart.

Sniper Team 6 came back and said, "Roger that, Hulk. I have a visual on the launchers; they've just launched from a back garden."

"Sniper 6, take the shot," commanded Stuart.

Thirty seconds later the radio crackled to life again, "Sniper 6, Sniper 6, do you copy, Hulk?"

"Roger, Sniper 6. Hulk copies. Go," said Stuart.

"Roger, Hulk. Confirm two casualties, both down," reported Sniper Team 6.

The radio came alive again as the sound of the air force pilots came through, "Angels, Angels, this is Cyclone 1. Confirm we have intercepted the missile; say again, confirm we have intercepted the missile. It had gone live, but we distributed our resources and have been able to destroy it."

"Roger that. And thanks, Cyclone 1."

The words were hardly out of Stuart's mouth when the radio crackled to life again, "This is Cyclone 7 to Angels. We have a launch; say again, we have a launch at Gatwick."

"Roger that," said Stuart. "Angels, do you have confirmation of the launch site? Do any of our snipers have eyes on?"

"Negative, negative," said Angels 2. "But we have been able to identify the block where the launch originated. We have our teams moving in to start sweeping now." Within the next few minutes the battle radio net came alive as the reports started to flood in.

Angels 2 came up on the net, "Hulk, Hulk, do you copy?"

"Angels 2, this is Hulk. Go!" said Stuart

"Roger, Hulk. We have found the launch group; unfortunately they put up a fight, and we had to neutralise them both. I say again, we have two confirmed hostiles dead," said Angels 2.

"Roger that. Thank you, Angels 2. So... we know we've got the groups here. Start to uplift the teams; get the bodies down for intel to ID." Stuart paused for just a moment, then got back on the radio, "Angels 3, Angels 3, do you copy?"

Angels three was the group that had been tasked with looking after Manchester. "Roger, Hulk, this is Angels 3. Do you have any intel for me?"

"Negative at this time, Angels 3. We have been checking passenger manifests, but have not identified anything at this time. We have Cyclone overhead ready to assist you, but have no positive info at this time," said Hulk. "I can be on my way to you within the next hour. Standby. Will see you then."

Stuart turned just as Tom made his way through the door. "Hulk, job well done. We've got both teams of extremists down."

Stuart turned to Tom and said, "Son, you all did a great job. I need to make my way up to Angels 3 within the next hour. I want you to pull the guys back to base in Cornwall. The SAS will handle the mopping up operations here and maintain a presence just in case we missed some crazy."

"Roger that," Tom said. Making his way across to the Hulk aka Stuart, he put his arms around him and said, "Dad, just remember I love you. It has been a tough day. But although civilians died as well as one of our own guys, we got the guys that did it before they could kill again. We just need to trust God; He will bring us through this."

Stuart patted Tom on the back and said, "I know that son, but it doesn't stop the anger and pain."

~~~~~

Manchester
20h00 hours

Stuart sat across the table from the Angel 3 commander. "Any news?" he asked.

"Negative," said the Angels 3 leader.

The words were hardly out of his mouth when the radio came alive and one of the spotters said, "We have a launch! We have a launch! Confirm we have a launch."

Stuart barked into the radio, "Do you have a visual confirmed?"
~~~~~

"Roger that" said Sniper 2. "We have a visual; engaging now."

A few minutes later the radio came back to life, "Angels 3, Angels 3, Sniper 2, do you copy?"

Angels 3 commander came on the net and said, "Roger. Copy. Go."

"Roger, Angels 3. We have definite confirmation... 2 kills down; we've got them," reported Sniper Team 2.

Angels 3 commander looked across at Stuart and said, "So that's it."

At the same time the radio came to life and Cyclone came up and said, "Angels, Angels, Cyclone November; you copy?"

"Roger, Cyclone November. This is Angels 3. Go."

"Just to confirm our boys intercepted the missile; they deployed their resources and the missile was destroyed."

"Roger that, Cyclone. Thanks so much for the assist. Please tell your boys, 'Well done from the brown jobs.' Now we can wrap this up; let's get those boys home to bed."

"Roger that, Angels 3. Same to you; job well done. Thanks so much," replied the Cyclone Commander.

As the radio died, Stuart turned round to his team and said, "Guys, really proud of you. This is a wrap. Let's head home; we've got a lot of planning to do."

CHAPTER THIRTEEN

SAF Base Cornwall
2 months later

Stuart stood on the hilltop overlooking the Special Assault Force base in Cornwall. His eyes swept to his left to the beautiful vista of the Cornish sea and the wonderful beach that the sea broke against; turning to his right, he could see the Special Assault Force base. Behind that lay the residency quarters of the officers and soldiers that made up the unit.

The past two months had been a time of frenetic activity: recruiting new members to the unit, training, and fortifying the camp against any possible attack. Stuart's eyes swept across to the new posts that had been put up around the camp. To the uninformed eye they just looked like huge, empty rugby posts, but strung between each one of them was what appeared to be almost sail-like structures. These were special anti-rocket curtains that could be dropped in the event of attack, forming a curtain – that if hit by the rockets – would cause them to explode.

All around the camp special, high-tech defence mechanisms had been put in place to deal with the advent of any attack. With the events of the past months, the special assault force unit had garnered a lot of high profile publicity. And especially in the eyes of the extremist Jihadi warriors, they were definitely public enemy number one. Stuart had no doubt that sooner or later there would be some form of reprisal against them.

Stuart felt tremendous pride in his unit; they had accomplished so much in such a short time. He felt so compelled right at that moment that he got down on his knees in the lush green grass of Cornwall and took the time to bow his head and pray and thank God for all that He had done – for His hand of protection and for the fact that they were just so confident that God was moving with them.

As Stuart finished his prayer and rose from his knees, he was overcome again with an overwhelming sense of impending doom, a spirit of unease almost like evil was hovering just at the gate again, waiting to step in and once again claim lives.

Stuart slowly made his way down the hill and walked through the door of the operations room. He turned to Tom, his son and the commander of the Angels 1 detachment, and said to him, "Tom, please meet me in my office in about five minutes."

He then made his way across to his intel team, led by the newly promoted Major Roy (Bugs) Franks. There had also been a new addition to the intelligence team – a new captain in the form of Captain Storm Ireland, aka the Countess of St Ives. Stuart's daughter had been a welcome asset to the team, bringing the very analytical brain that she had inherited from her father to play in the different operations that they had been involved in.

Stuart turned to Bugs and said, "Bugs, I want the guards doubled. I want thermal imaging equipment to be running at top performance. I want our drones to be out there scouting. I want our radar to alert me of any ships that come any closer than two or three kilometres to the base. I've just got this real sense that God's communicating that we need to be ready. Tell all our personnel, including those that have been allocated to standby, that I want them ready to go at a moment's notice."

Stuart then turned on his heel and made his way into his office. Closing the door he turned round to Tom and said, "Tom, take the weight off your feet." Tom sank into one of the comfortable, green leather, easy chairs that Stuart had furnished his office with.

"Tom, I received a communication this morning. My recommendation that you be promoted to full colonel and take command of the Special Assault Force has been accepted.

"My role as we move forward is going to be that of overall commander of the different Special Force units that we are slowly starting to join together and develop as a cohesive fighting force against these particular threats as they arise. So, my job will be to oversee this unit, the SAS and the other units that we are adding. Joe is going to be the SAS colonel in charge, and Rob will be my 2IC. He will step in and take control of the operations should something happen to me."

Stuart looked across at his son affectionately and said, "Well done, Tom. You've really done well in the time that we have been operating, and the way that you've lead your men is exemplary. But we really need to prepare ourselves now; I feel very strongly that it's now time for us to start to move on the intel we've been getting. Could you please call a briefing of all the Angels commanders. We also need to bring in the commanders from the SAS, as well as the commanders from the special units that we've earmarked from the Royal Marines and some of the other units. Please have all the commanders here tomorrow at 09:00 for a briefing."

"Roger that, Hulk," said Dude. "I'll get that sorted out."

Tom rose to his feet, came smartly to attention and saluted his dad. As he started to make his way towards the door, Stuart called after him and said, "Don't forget to get your badges of rank changed; I'll be informing all our troops in the next hour or so about the changes."

~~~~~

Later that evening as the sun sank just below the horizon, Stuart was sitting around the table with Jane completing the evening meal, when he suddenly stood to his feet and said, "Jane, I've got a go. I've just really got this compulsion that I need to be out there tonight with our standby troops. I feel deeply
~~~~~

that something's going to be going down; it's as if God is compelling me to get the guys ready."

Stuart exited his bungalow and made his way the short distance up the road, through the gate and into the operational part of the base. He made his way smartly across to the operations room. As always, Bugs was on duty; it seemed like he never slept. Turning to him Stuart said, "Bugs, please bring the guys to standby alert; I want the guys to be manning the defences this evening. I'm running on a God-hunch here that something is going to be going down tonight."

"Roger that, Sir," said Bugs as he reached across to pick up the radio and send out the call.

Stuart thought for a moment and then said, "Bugs, ask the second-tier standby to be ready, too. Also, I want gunships to be on the helipad, warmed up and ready to go should the need arise. Let's have Popeye in position, and, Bugs, I want your drones out there in force tonight."

Bugs smiled. The drones were the latest addition to the unit's capabilities; they had proved to be a huge help in the follow up of the missile attacks that had taken place at Heathrow, and they were his special project. He loved them, and Stuart was coming to love them too, because they were bringing to the unit a unique aspect of being able to seek out and have early warning of things that were developing. They were also able to keep an eye on what was happening on the ground.

Special Assault Force Base, Cornwall
23:00 hours

Stuart, kitted out in full combat gear, was standing on the hill overlooking the beach. Around him were twenty of his best men; they were all camoed up and had merged with the darkness of the still night. The clouds, which were fairly thick, hung in the air like pregnant ducks, slow-moving, keeping that deep and impenetrable curtain of pitch black darkness just hanging over the landscape.

The radio came alive, "Hulk, Hulk, do you copy? This is Bugs. Do you copy?"

Stuart reached down and touched his throat mike, "Roger, Bugs. Copy. What have you got for me?"

"Hulk, it seems like you were right. We've got two freighters on the radar. I've tasked two satellites overhead, and they are bringing us images of two freighter boats, registered to Libya, making their way towards the beach below. They are about two miles out now."

"Roger. Thanks, Bugs. Let's bring everybody to full alert; I think we may well be in business tonight," replied Stuart.

23:45 hours

The freighters had now made their way much closer to the beach; and if the natural human eye could penetrate the deepening darkness, the soldiers would have seen the scramble nets being dropped down the side and the rigid inflatable boats being lowered into the water. Their propellers feathered for stealth, the RIBs began to fill with men; soon, upwards of 120 men were being ferried between the freighters and the beach.

Unbeknown to them, their every move was being closely monitored overhead. One of Bugs' drones, a specially developed drone called 'The Owl' – so named for its ability to fly with almost undetectable sound and equipped with thermal imagery – was at this moment feeding back the thermal pictures as the men clambered off the trawlers into the RIBs. They made their way to the beach; once gathered, they quickly split off into different sections and began to make their way up the paths.

Stuart, now with his thermal night vision goggles on, turned to his men and said, "Right, guys, we are in business. This part of the coast is a no-go area, so it is most definitely hostiles that are coming in."

Stuart pushed his throat mike again, activated it to permanently on and said, "Bugs, you copy?"

"Roger, Hulk. Copy," came back the reply.

"Right, Bugs, drop the anti-rocket nets please. And send out the call to all the staff quarters; I want all lights out. I don't want the hostiles identifying any easy targets should any of them break through."

"Roger that, Hulk," said Bugs as he swiftly moved to put the order into action.

Slowly and surely the figures from the beach stealthily made their way up through the gorse and the paths which wound between the gorse, gradually reaching the point where they started to crest the rise; there, in the valley below, the camp was nestled, seemingly asleep and unaware of the impending danger.

The attackers would have high-ground advantage, which they thought would give them the element of surprise. Like so many of the different extremist movements, their fervour had limited their diagnostic abilities – the strategic abilities to be able to realise that the force they were about to attack had been the force that had repeatedly outwitted them time and time again. A force made up of men and woman who were highly trained. But not only that. In this force, every single member was a born-again believer; they were men and women who relied not only on their own skills and weaponry, but as a unit relied on the leading and protection from God.

It was this leading and prompting from God that had warned Stuart that something was about to happen tonight.

One of the dark shapes lifted something to his shoulder; Stuart could see very clearly through his night goggles that this was an RPG rocket. As the intruder lifted his rocket towards his shoulder, Stuart gave the command, "This is a go. Go! Go! Activate Operation Lockdown now!"

As those words left his mouth, the night sky came alive with the blast of heavy machine gun fire. The tracer rounds swept across the landscape; laser-controlled robotic machine gun posts seemed to pop up out of the gorse, the heavy bullets starting to tear into the area where the intruders had gathered. The machine gun fire was closely followed by the staggered explosions of the deadly claymore mines and other ordinances that had been placed there by the defensive team. Within seconds the night was transformed as the blasts, accompanied by the heavy fire power, poured down onto the intruders. Their screams of pain, anguish and frustration carried across the night sky.

Stuart spoke into his radio, "Release the Hawks for hunting."

In response, Stuart heard the softly muted tones of the four attack helicopters that rose from the helipad sweeping overhead and making their way towards the two freighters that had anchored offshore. As they swept down towards the freighters, the rotors were so muted that those on board – hearing dulled by the noise of the sea and the blasts on the land – never even heard them coming. As they closed in like the birds of prey that they were named after, the Hawks released their deadly ordinances as missiles streaked out through the dark night sky towards the two trawlers. The trawlers erupted in a burst of flame, followed soon after by massive explosions as their own fuel sources ignited.

Stuart, looking across at the two balls of fire a short way offshore, was fairly confident that with the mass of ordinance that had poured into the ships and the two balls of fire that had erupted, there wouldn't be any survivors.

Down below him the defence systems in the defence units were doing their job. Stuart spoke again, "Robotic armaments, cease fire." The mass assault of the machine gun fire fell silent. Down below, only screams of pain were heard; most of the intruders had started to run back towards the beach only to discover that the trawlers offshore were now just balls of flame. As they started to scramble into their RIBs, the Hawks sprung again. Sweeping over the shoreline, machine gun fire and multiple rockets spewed out from the helicopters, totally annihilating and destroying the RIBs that were on the beach.

Stuart spoke and said, "Stop groups, mop up."

Teams came sweeping from out of the blackness as bunker lids popped. The specially constructed defence bunkers that had been put in place were undetectable to the untrained eye, undetectable in most cases even to the trained eye. Out of them poured specialised units, men and women trained in the art of stealth movement. They closed rapidly on what was now just a small handful of survivors, no more than fifteen to twenty, who were now stranded on the beach; like a circle of steel, the Angels started to enclose them.

A voice broke through the darkness. Tom's voice.

"Lay down your arms and surrender, and none of you will be hurt."

The intruders looked around at the devastation – their comrades lying all around them in various stages of death, many of the survivors completely shattered, not physically, but emotionally and mentally. What they had just seen, the devastation of the firepower and the way their comrades had been so speedily and quickly dispatched, filled them with dread. All along the beach arms went into the air; AK-47s and rocket launchers clattered to the ground, falling with a soft muted thud into the sand and the occasional sharper clang as they struck a rock.

Stuart gave another command, "Icarus, on."

Suddenly, the beach was bathed in huge spotlights, spotlights carefully concealed up on the surrounding hills. The intruders were now very clearly visible to the naked eye. They were young men, heads wrapped in shemaghs. Jihadi warriors swept up and brainwashed by the rantings of their fanatical Imams, men twisted by hate – a hate that had appealed to these young men, had offered them a life of excitement and adventure, but had instead led them into an ambush.

Tom and his men moved down, quickly securing the intruders; medical staff followed soon after. But of the tremendous number of bodies scattered around, there were only three that they were able to work on. The remote heavy machine guns, claymores and other ordinance that had been deployed had done the deadly work they were designed for.

Stuart spoke into his mike again, "Popeye 1, Popeye 1, do you copy?"

His radio crackled back to life. "Roger, Hulk. This is Popeye 1," came the reply.

"Popeye 1, please confirm. Have you picked up any survivors?' Stuart queried.

Popeye 1 manned the Rigid Inflatables Boats, RIBs, that belonged to the Special Assault Force. Some of them had been sitting offshore in clandestine mode, waiting in case they were needed.

"Negative. Negative, Hulk. The freighters both sank. No survivors. I say again, no survivors."

"Roger that, Popeye 1. Thank you; you can return to base," ordered Stuart.

"Roger that, Hulk. Popeye 1 out," came the acknowledgement.

Stuart, together with two other operators, made their way down onto the beach. The attackers lay on their stomachs hands firmly secured behind them.

"Get them onto their knees," Stuart commanded, his eyes running over the remnants of the Jihadi force that had come to seek their vengeance on the Special Assault Force, had come to seek their vengeance on the Angels, only to find that the Angels were not an easy group to kill, that the Angels were themselves a group of fearsome warriors, made up of men and women highly skilled and highly trained.

Dude made his way across to Stuart, "Hulk, I can confirm we have 21 confirmed captives; the men have swept through, and the body count is 105. That may change as some of them were pretty badly hit by the explosion. I expect we will only have a definitive number once we can operate in the daylight. There is a lot of work to be done to piece everything together."

Stuart grinned at the unintended pun, "Roger that, Dude; just keep me informed." He then walked across and looked into the faces of the young Jihadi warriors; most of them looked like scared schoolboys, suddenly caught up in a situation that they had never dreamed possible. But now reality had caught up with them.

Stuart came and stood in front of them, and his eyes swept across the group. Catching the eyes of every single one of them, he started to speak, "Yes, it's easy to attack people who aren't armed; it's easy to attack men, women, children, babies and old people who can't defend themselves. You've been made to feel big and invincible. Well, welcome to the real world. Yes, welcome to reality. Because tonight, you came not to attack defenceless men and women and children and babies; tonight you came to attack some of the very best soldiers in the world."

Stuart looked each one of them in the eye again, catching them in his compelling gaze, holding them. Not one of them could drop their eyes, almost as if they were is mesmerised by the magnetic stare that Stuart had locked on them. He spoke again, "Look around you. Look at all your dead comrades. Look at them and remember that real war against real soldiers is not a game; you cannot push the reboot button and have them come back to life. In real war when you die, you stay dead."

At Stuart's words tears began to form in the eyes of many of the young men and then fall down their cheeks, as they realised the horror and the gravity of the situation they found themselves in.

Again, Stuart locked his eyes with theirs and said, "Many of you will spend the rest of your life in prison, never knowing or having wives or children. No joy. You will spend your lives in solitary confinement – no TV, no computer, no video games. You will be locked away year after year after year after year."

Stuart's steely gaze penetrated to the heart of these men that had come to kill – to kill not only soldiers but also kill the families of the soldiers, to kill their wives, to kill their children, to kill their new-born babies.

"BUT...," continued Stuart. Many of the young Jihadi warriors' heads came up, and hope flickered in their eyes.

"But *if* you cooperate and *if* we are convinced that you are cooperating fully, there may be some degree of the leniency in your sentencing. You will still spend a long time in prison, but maybe your conditions will be better."

Having planted that seed, that tiny kernel of hope in the midst of the deep despair they were feeling, Stuart swung on his heel and turned to Tom and said,

"Right, Dude, get them up to the holding cells. Give them a good meal, and then first thing in the morning we start the interrogation."

~~~~~

SAF Briefing Room
09:00 hours

Stuart glanced around the conference table. Seated in the room were the commanders of the Special Assault Force, the commanders of the Special Air Services, some commanders from certain detachments of the Royal Marines, and various other commanders from the Air Force and the Navy – a unique mix that had been gathered together by Stuart to form the backbone of the Assault Strike Force.

Stuart turned to them all saying, "Right, chaps. You know what took place last night; you know that we were the object of a direct attack by Islamic militants. They sought to gain entrance to our base to hurt us as a unit. And also hurt our families. They have once again shown that they are totally unscrupulous, that they are prepared to attack innocent civilians as well as soldiers. That means, ladies and gentlemen, that we are going to step up our activity. Up until now we've remained within our
~~~~~

borders. We have played a protection role. We have played a containment role.

"But these Islamic extremists are being harboured and hosted in countries all over the world. The intel that is coming from the different interrogations of the various people that we have rounded up informs us that they have got sympathetic governments all over the world that are working with them. Some of those governments are working with them because they are in agreement with the particular extremist beliefs and are united in their hatred towards the Western world. Some are working with the extremists because of the profit that it brings and the embedded levels of corruption within individual governments. But from where we stand, the reasons are immaterial.

"We now need to start to take the fight to these particular groups in the countries where they are being harboured, and if necessary even take the fight to the leaders of the countries that are harbouring them. Should they get in our way or seek to stop us, we will deal with them too."

"Any questions so far?" Stuart asked.

Not one hand went up, but it was very clear, looking at all the faces around the table, that the group was very determined. These were men and women who were trained to do the job, men and women who had made a violent oath to protect their country – a country that was now under threat, and they were ready to take the fight to the enemy.

"Right, guys, let's give you a quick overview. But remember, what you hear here is top secret. It is not to be mentioned beyond the walls of this room until you get the go-ahead to begin briefing your men and women on the ground.

"We are looking for a coordinated attack on the particular bases that the extremists have set up in the different countries. Because of Tom's and my expertise in Southern Africa and our knowledge of the area, we will be handling the operations in that region. We currently have intel that suggests the four countries that are actively working with these Islamic extremists are South Africa, Zimbabwe, Mozambique and Zambia. The intel that we've gleaned shows that they have not only provided the Jihadists with resources to set up the training camp, but that they are also providing them with resources in terms of identification books, passports etc – in essence, everything that they need to be able to pass through into different parts of the world undetected from the point of origin.

"Our estimates are that the camps range in size from between 100 and 150, with up to 800 in some cases. The major camps are located in South Africa and Zimbabwe, with smaller camps in Zambia and Mozambique. Gentlemen, ladies, we need to eradicate this particular threat. Our logistics team has been working on a number of feasible plans that will get us on-site and help us to be able to do the unique job that is required. I'm going to be relying on every single one of you to help us accomplish the mission that we have before us.

"Right, guys, let's step outside for a little bit of a demonstration."

They rose and left the conference room and followed Hulk up towards the firing range. Once there he spoke into his radio and said, "Right, guys, the demonstration can commence."

At the far end of the one firing range, a number of life-sized dummies popped up. As the commanders watched, there was a faint hiss in the air; and then, before their eyes, the drone that was called 'The Owl' appeared. It was a small drone, no bigger than a dinner plate, and so silent that you could hardly hear it. It flew to a distance of about fifteen metres from the dummy, aligned itself – and then, those watching heard a short hiss and the dummy's head exploded.

Some of the commanders who hadn't seen this before asked, "What on earth is that?"

"That," said Bugs, "is our silent Owl drone. It is mounted with a 9mm calibre suppressed weapon, and each drone is capable of carrying five rounds. They can be aimed and aligned with a laser sight, and from a maximum distance of twenty metres can subdue a target. This is an excellent weapon that could be used to neutralise guards, because it has full night thermal imaging resources on board. As you can see, we have needed to develop some very unique technology to cover the different operations that we will be taking part in."

Stuart turned round to the commanders and said, "Now, in the field in front of you, fifteen men are concealed. I would like you to pick them out and identify their positions. You men are the elite of the elite; let's see how good you really are."

All the commanders scanned the area in front of them, among the gorse and the short grass. After five minutes of intense scrutiny, they all turned round to Stuart and said, "With all due respect, Sir, we don't believe there is anybody there. We cannot identify even one; you are pulling our leg."

Stuart spoke in his radio, "Angels 1, uncloak." And as if by some slight-of-hand trick, suddenly in front of the commanders, fifteen soldiers materialised at different positions in the gorse, the closest no more than five metres from them. The commanders were absolutely gobsmacked.

Stuart turned to them, a smile on his face, and said, "Gentlemen, we've heard about this technology that has been used in planes. We have been able to develop cloaking materials that will take on the properties of the area they are surrounded by — be it darkness, the surrounding vegetation, whatever — thus making men almost undetectable. It also has a special coating which helps to protect them from being identified on any type of thermal resource."

One of the SAS commanders turned round and said, "Sir, how long has this technology been available? Why has it not been made available to our units already?"

Stuart gave a chuckle and said, "Take it easy, Joe; this technology has only been made available in the last three weeks. It's been in the testing and development phase, so your unit was not overlooked or slighted. We've been able to recruit some of the really top smart minds, and they have been working on it for us.

"Gentlemen, ladies, we will be going into the situation carrying conventional arms, but with this type of technology, we will have a huge advantage. The cloaking means that we will be able to get up close and personal with the enemy.

"We will only get one shot at this. One shot! And we need to make sure that we put them all way once and for all! We must deliver such a decisive blow that it takes them a lifetime to recover from it."

Stuart turned and made his way back into the conference room; the balance of his commanders followed right behind.

"You have now seen some of the technology; there is more to come along the way... Right, let's look at some of the specifics of the missions. As previously mentioned, the men and women sitting around this table will be dealing with Southern Africa. The Americans have put together a similar strike force, and they are going to be dealing with the Middle East and some countries down in South America that have become very sympathetic to the Islamic extremists.

"The Russians have also put together a unit. We have been giving them intel, because they too are facing their own particular problems with the Islamic extremists, who are fast becoming a threat to the whole region. They will be dealing with some of the camps that have been set up in their particular patch."

Stuart turned to the Royal Marine contingents and said, "Gentlemen, your specific theatre of operation is going to be here in Europe. We have identified a number of small bases in countries in Europe, and you are the unit that has been tasked to deal with them. You will have elements of the SAS who will go with you and help you as you carry out your training for this mission.

The key element of these missions is that we have to hit them all at the same time. Gentlemen, these are the specifics of your mission."

For the next twelve hours, Stuart, Tom, Rob and Joe briefed the various commanders on the roles they would be playing. At about 22:00 hours that evening Stuart finally looked up and said, "Right, ladies and gentlemen, that's it."

As the commanders left, Stuart and Tom made their way down to the residential area of the camp. Stuart turned to Tom and said, "Tom, are you up for this?"

Tom looked across at his dad. He could see the fatigue written on Stuart's face; after all he wasn't a young man any more and the last few months had been full of action and a lot of stress.

"I'm up for it, Dad," said Tom. "You are the one I'm concerned about. Are you sure that you want to go on these raids? Are you sure that you wouldn't be better served sitting back here in the command post?"

Briefly Stuart's face hardened.

"No, Tom. I need to be on these raids; that's my old stomping ground, and there is unfinished business there as well. These countries that we know and love have started to harbour the enemy of our nation. And they are not doing so for any ideological reasons; they doing it for cold hard cash. Many of the people are starving and don't have running water or food on the table. But these fat cats are not only gorging themselves on the natural resources of the country; they are also involved in selling out to these extremists, assigning them safe haven purely for money."

Stuart turned to his son. "Tom, it sickens me when I think of all those people – hungry, homeless, no education – and yet an elite few gorge themselves like bloodsucking ticks at the expense of the people. Remember, in the mid-80s Robert Mudabe brought in the Korean Fifth Brigade, and they slaughtered and massacred the Matabele. Mudabe may appear to be an aged gentleman now, but he is no gentleman; he is a vicious, cold-hearted killer who has been ruthless in stamping out anybody who sought to rise up against him, who spoke against him. And, Tom, we need to deal with him and that particular brood of vipers that he has cultivated. We need to take him down as well as the camps."

Stuart looked around the conference room at the faces of his commanders.

"Right, ladies and gentlemen, this is the plan of operation. One detachment of SAS will move into Zambia; one detachment will move into Mozambique. Angels 1 and 2 will move into Zimbabwe, while Angels 3 and 4, together with 2 units of the SAS will deal with South Africa. Ladies and gentlemen, we have 48 hours in order to make this operation become a reality once we have boots on the ground. Any questions?"

Hands shot up all over the room as the commanders sought reassurance of final details, recapping small points to make sure they had everything in place. Stuart looked around at his men and women and said, "Right guys and girls, this is a go. Get your kit ready. Say goodbye to your families. We fly out at 21:00 hours this evening. Let's go, team! It's thumping time."

~~~~~

Stuart looked across at Jane as they sat down for their final meal together before Stuart left for his mission. Tension and worry were etched on Jane's face. Stuart reached across the table to gather both of her hands in his and said, "Don't worry, Love. God
~~~~~

will go before us; He will be our strength and our shield."

"I know that," said Jane, "but I can't help feeling afraid for you and Tom and the other troops in the unit. You are going into a very dangerous situation."

Stuart stood up, made his way round to Jane's side of the table and lifted her out of her chair. He gathered her into his arms, and tilting her head gently, he looked into her eyes and said, "Love, know this. I love you more than life itself, but should God ordain – and it would be his ordaining to take my life – know this: one day we will meet again, because death does not have its sting."

The tears slowly gathered at the corner of Jane's eyes and began to run; she just hung onto her husband and said, "Stuart, you know I love you. We have been through so much together since you swept me off my feet so many years ago, and the thought of life without you… it's almost unimaginable."

Stuart hugged his wife close and whispered into her ear. "Jane, you know I feel exactly the same way. You have been my heartbeat; you have been my soulmate. Love, as we agreed that day after the Perranporth attack, God has called me for such a time as this… Let's pray together and ask God to cover us and to be with both of us, with our loved ones. And with the men and women who go and those who stay behind."

Jane and Stuart quietly knelt down together and moved into communion with their King and Lord, Jesus Christ.

~~~~~

Across the road in a bungalow not far away, Tom was looking into Trish's eye. Trish's face was also filled with worry and fear, much as Jane's face had been. Tom gathered up his little son, Sam, who was running around as usual. He then reached out with his other arm to pull Trish close to his side. "Darling, don't worry; God is with us. We've got a job to do, and we need to get it done now."

Trish looked at her husband, the man she had loved since she was a six-year-old girl. Images flashed across her mind – following him around at church, at school, always managing to be in the background, always managing to be a part of his life. Until one day he grew up and suddenly realised that she was 'the one', and the thought of her not being there had filled him with despair and revealed his true love for her.

Trish looked at this man whom she loved so much. As she thought of what an excellent husband and father he was, her heart swelled with love and gratitude. "Tom," she said, "I've got some news for you. I wasn't going to tell you until you came back... but I have to." She grabbed hold of Tom and looked up into his eyes and said, "Hon, I'm pregnant. We are going to have another baby."
~~~~~

Tom's face came alight with pure joy. He pulled his wife even closer and gave her mind-blowing kiss. "Honey, I am so excited! That is such good news!"

Reaching down, he once again grabbed hold of little Sam, who had escaped from his grasp, and tossed him in the air. "Sam, you are going to have a little brother or sister!"

Sam let out a squeal of joy. He loved it when his dad played with him. He loved it when his dad wrestled with him. And now he loved the idea that he was getting a new brother or sister. As he cuddled into his dad's arms, he turned to his mom and said, "Are we going out to the shop to pick up my new brother or sister?"

Trish laughed and said, "Oh, Sam, in about seven months' time, the Lord Jesus will give us your little brother or sister. Tomorrow, Mommy will explain how babies grow."

Sam looked across at his mommy and said, "Oh, Mom, me know where babies grow; they grow in their mommies' tummies. We see lots of ladies around the base who have babies growing in their tummies."

Trish and Tom laughed. "Well, so much for our early lecture on the birds and the bees; it seems he's pretty much got it sorted himself," said Tom before reaching across and taking Trish back into his arms to complete the family circle. "Let's pray as a family," he said.

As the prayer ended, Tom sat down with little Sam and said, "Sam, Daddy will be gone from home for a little while. I want you to know that Daddy loves you and cares for you. And while Daddy is gone, the Lord Jesus is going to look after you and Mommy."

~~~~~

Stuart exited his bungalow and made his way across to another bungalow further down the street. This was where his daughter, Storm, and her husband, Steve, lived. Storm was now a captain in the logistics division of the Special Assault Force; Steve was a young trainee preparing to go through the rigorous selection course required for admission into the Special Assault Force. In addition to working on his fitness, Steve was getting basic training in weaponry and various other skills that he would be required to have.

Stuart knocked on the door, which opened quickly. He stepped through the door and looked at Storm and Steve and said, "I've just come to say goodbye."

Suddenly, into the room erupted a little fireball of energy. It was Stuart's granddaughter, his oldest grandchild, Michelle. With a squeal upon seeing her granddaddy, she rocketed across the room and launched herself into his arms; he picked her up and swung her around and said, "How you doing, Sweet Pea?"

Michelle was a bubbly child — so full of energy, so full of the joy of living and yes, also the noisiest grandchild that he had. Stuart put her gently
~~~~~

back down on her feet, then turned round to Storm and said, "I've really just come to say goodbye and ask you to keep an eye on your Mom and Trish."

Looking across the room at Steve, Stuart continued, "Steve, it's your job to look after the ladies now. Just make sure you do it well."

Steve smiled. He was looking slim and trim and was following a rigorous fitness regime in preparation for running selection course. "Don't worry, Dad, I'll keep my eye on them and make sure they are safe. We will be praying for you guys every day, trusting that God will keep you safe."

Stuart stepped forward and gathered all three into his arms. "Just know I love you all... Let's pray."

Together they bowed their heads and sought God's blessing and protection for the days ahead.

CHAPTER FOURTEEN

Forty-eight hours later, in the airspace over southern Africa and at different altitudes all in excess of twenty thousand feet, various airliners were flying, crossing over Zimbabwe, Mozambique, South Africa and Zambia. They appeared to be normal passenger airliners; but as the aircrafts crossed over specific locations in each of the four countries, their pressurised cargo-hold doors opened and from each one was deployed what appeared to be three capsules, each about half the size of a sea-going container.

As the capsules fell free from the aircraft, parachutes were deployed above them and they continued to fall until they were about two thousand feet above ground. At that point, what appeared to be some sort of thruster mechanism kicked in, slowing their rate of descent and bringing them to a standstill on the ground with almost feather-light precision.

From within one of the three containers released over Zimbabwe, Major 'Bugs' Franks gave a big grin as he turned to the operators who shared his container and said, "See; I told you it would work."

A rather pale fellow operator looked at him and gave a wry smile. "Sir," he said, "if it had not worked, then we would have been squashed like a bug on the tarmac... if you will excuse the pun."

Laughter broke out in the module; the very weak joke had broken the tension, and the men in the module were beginning to breathe normally again after a period of high anxiety.

Simultaneous with the deployment of the containers, 'regular' airliners at an altitude even higher opened pressurised cargo holds to release a stream of men and women all dressed for HALO – high altitude, low opening – parachute drops. They fell away into the dark night sky, also deploying their parachutes just before the ground and steering in the last three thousand feet with absolute precision.

Within twenty minutes, in each of the four countries, the three containers were fully operational. In one of them was a full mini field hospital; in another a full communications and operations room; and in the last, which was set up with a line with of seats and consoles, were well-trained drone operators, many of them highly-skilled, successful gamers whom Stuart had recruited. The many drones would play a critical role in the success of the whole operation.

Stuart came up on the radio as he called into the different units in the various countries. The replies came back quickly; the descent and landing had been free of any problems in each of the four key locations. In Zambia they had landed to the east of Kabwe, very close to the border with Mozambique and Malawi; that's where intel suggested the Jihadi camp was based. In Zimbabwe they had landed very close to what was known as Rusambo village – close to the spot where the Old Catholic Mission used to be and where the Jihadi camp was now based. The group in Mozambique had landed to the east of Nampula; and in South Africa, the forces had landed to the east of Punda Maria, in the world renowned Kruger National Park, close to the border with Mozambique.

In each of the four specified locations, the special force operators quickly set up the communications; all was ready by 23:00 hours. Stuart then deployed his scouts to move in and begin close quarter's reconnaissance of the bases that they would be attacking.

They had specifically picked a night where there was no moon; it was incredibly dark, and the special force troops quickly moved out and began to follow the initial reconnaissance units that had gone before. Soon Stuart and his Angels Group found themselves lying outside the Jihadi camp that was now based at the site of the Old Catholic Mission. To the north-east were two small mountains with a saddle between them; to the west lay a small dam.

Stuart knew this area well. As a young soldier doing his National Service in the Rhodesian Bush War, he had served out of the camp that was based at that time in the old Roman Catholic Mission. He had been one recipient of an infamous attack, which had been launched from within the saddle between the two hills.

The Angels lay in the darkness, the night imaging equipment giving them absolute clarity of what was going down on the ground. They could make out that it was a fairly sizeable base. Stuart turned to Tom and said, "I estimate we could be dealing with between six to eight hundred hostiles."

"Hulk," replied Tom, "look at the guards; they are so lax. They've got no more than twelve guards out around the camp, which for this size is far too few. And look, they are not being attentive; they're not even facing outwards, just smoking and joking with each other. And in that guard tower over there, they're listening to the radio."

Stuart followed Tom's gaze, then turned to him and said, "Well, we need to realise that they feel quite safe in this part of southern Africa; they have, to a large extent, been protected by the various governments that make up the establishment."

Stuart put out a call on his radio, "Bugs, do you copy? Hulk here."

Bugs immediately came up on the net. "Roger, Hulk, I copy fives," responded Bugs.

"Bugs, we are ready to implement the assault operation; let's go to phase one," said Stuart.

"Roger that," said Bugs. "Out."

Phase one of the operation involved Bugs bringing in his Owl drones, each one of them controlled by an operator set up in the container-like drone centre specifically designed for them. The little Owl drones swooped in, hardly making a sound. Within a matter of minutes, each one of them was strategically positioned close to a guard. Stuart spoke into his radio and gave the 'go' order to his operators. A faint hissing sound reached their tuned ears, the sounds of the shots muted by the special technology and venting port systems that have been incorporated into the Owls' weaponry, Special flash hiders hid the flame as the 9mm rounds each found their mark. The guards, who should have been alerting their comrades to any form of attack, now lay slumped on the ground. Simultaneously, black shadows slipped out from the surrounding bush.

Stuart came back up on the battle net. "Hulk here; implement operation cloak."

Where moments before there seemed to be black shadows, there were now no shadows as Hulk and his special operators began to employ the special cloaking technology that had been developed. Each one of their battle suits incorporated the cloaking technology, their heads encased in high-tech, lightweight, breathable balaclavas also incorporating the technology. It was almost as if they had become invisible. And in the eyes of the enemy, that was pretty much what had happened; the only giveaway was an occasional, slight ripple on what appeared to be the picture in front of them.

The Angels moved quickly into the camp, closely monitored and followed by Bugs' Owl drones. They moved through the camp, laying explosives and putting up identification posts that would come into play later in the operation. They also silently pushed a number of transport buses clear of the camp.

One of Bugs' drones made its way towards the main hall, coming in and hovering in one of the open windows, recording everything it 'saw' for later review. Bugs' monitors clearly revealed that there were in excess of six hundred men and women in the hall – all of them young, all of them with eyes riveted on another fairly young man, who was walking up and down the raised platform in front of them, ranting and raving as from his lips poured streams of hate and venom. Against the West. Against the Christians. Against anybody who did not hold to his particular extremist Islamic stance. As Bugs watched him through the screen, he heard him start to slate even those who were the 'moderate' Muslims, those who did not believe in the extremist position; he heard the young leader up at the front say, "These too are our enemies, and they must be annihilated and destroyed!"

It was very clear, just from the small snippet that Bugs had seen and heard, that what these young people were being indoctrinated with was an extremely aggressive, almost cancer-like, acidic brand of Islamic extremism that was designed to burn into the minds of the impressionable youth and turn them into young men and women who would have no compulsion about killing. Killing the innocent. Killing anybody who did not prescribe to their particular twisted brand of ideology.

Stuart's voice came over the radio, "Roger, guys, Hulk here. All explosives are in place; please withdraw to your predetermined positions."

Like ghosts in the darkness, which they effectively were with the cloaking technology, the special operators withdrew to positions about five hundred metres away from the camp.

Stuart pushed his intercom. "Initiate phase three," he commanded.

Overhead were a number of Predator drones that had been launched from an aircraft carrier sitting off of the Mozambique coast in the Mozambique Channel. These were specially adapted Predator drones with long-range capabilities, controlled by Bugs and his team of operators. Out of the dark sky of Zimbabwe came the 'Whispering Death' as the Predator drones swept down, each one of them locking onto the target indicator posts that had been put up in the camp by the operators earlier that night. Each one of them was placed in a strategic area that, together with explosives, would maximise the casualty rate, would maximise the destruction. The object of this mission was to eradicate this extremism cancer once and for all in order to secure the borders of the United Kingdom from attack by these radicals, radicals who had been harboured and succoured within these various countries.

At the same time, an almost carbon copy of what was taking place in Zimbabwe was unfolding in Zambia, Mozambique and South Africa. The other units that had been deployed were also going to phase three. In all four locations, the Predator drones swept down and unleashed their awesome firepower on the designated spots; this was simultaneously linked with the detonation of the substantial amount of ordinances that had been placed in what had become defenceless camps once the Owl drones had done their work and eliminated the sentries.

Within a matter of seconds, what had been thriving camps of young Jihadi idealists and extremists – men and women twisted by their rabid beliefs – now became blazing infernos, places that resembled the very pits of Hell itself. The sheer volume of explosives and other ordinances created such fireballs, such curtains of death, that it appeared impossible for anybody to survive them.

As the sounds of the explosions died, Stuart gave the command for phase four to begin. Out of the darkness, the operators, armed with their US-built Mod17 0 Scar rifles and Sig Sauer P239 side arms, swept into what was now the burning ruin of the extremist camp in Zimbabwe. Stuart led the way as his men swept through the camp; and although it was almost impossible to comprehend, some from within the camp had survived and opened fire on the operators.

They immediately went to cloaking again and systematically worked their way through the camp, mopping up and despatching any resistance that was found. Within half an hour every extremist Jihadi warrior had been eliminated.

"Roger," said Stuart as he came up on the battle net. "This is Hulk; implement phase five."

Phase five involved all the operators pulling back to where the three container-like modules were. Once assembled, they stripped off their combat gear which was quickly stowed in their battle bags and loaded into the containers. They changed into everyday clothes, similar to those worn by the Jihadi Warriors; each one of them was draped in a shemagh, skin darkened with the special chemical creams that they had applied at the beginning of the operation. From a distance – and even from up close – many of them would appear to be Jihadi warriors.

In the initial phase of the operation, the operators had silently, so as not to alert anyone, moved out four buses that had been used within the camp. These buses now stood at the side of the road outside the camp ready for use. Stuart's gaze swept across the hills and the saddle; he knew it would probably be only a few hours before the authorities would be looking from them. He turned to Bugs and asked, "Bugs, are we all good to go?"

Bugs nodded, "Yes, Hulk, all packed up and ready to inflate."

"Roger that," said Stuart. "Let's go to phase six."

Phase six of the operation involved inflating massive weather balloons. Attached to these balloons were three cables, which were in turn attached to the three modules. As the weather balloons inflated and rose up into the sky, they pulled the cables up with them, each cable linked by secondary cable to each of the other modules. From out of the dark night sky came the drone of an engine, faint because of the altitude it was flying at. As the weather balloons rose bringing up the initial cables followed by the secondary cables, a large transport plane swept by. Its arrester hook dangling below caught the cables, quickly winding them up; and within seconds the three modules lifted off the ground and could be seen dangling in the sky, rapidly gaining altitude as the carrier plane started to climb. Within a matter of minutes, it was as if there had been no modules there whatsoever.

Stuart's operators quickly swept the area with branches and leaves; it wouldn't fool an experienced tracker, but somebody would have to be looking very hard to discover that the modules had ever been there.

"Right, chaps," said Stuart, "let's make our way to the buses." In Rusambo, Stuart and his operators boarded their buses and made the short journey to the Mozambique border, crossing from Zimbabwe into Mozambique to the south of Tete.

In the other three locations very similar events were simultaneously unfolding. In Zambia to the east of Kabwe, very close to the border with Mozambique, the attack force boarded the buses and making their way towards the Mozambique border. In northern Mozambique to the east of Nampula, the operations group was similarly making its way towards the coast to the east; and in South Africa, the group that had taken out the big camp that was based just south of Punda Maria had likewise crossed into Mozambique with the buses and were making their way north of the Xai Xai district and then east towards the coast.

Stuart came up on the battle net and made an all units broadcast. "Well done, all, first class operation. Now let's get home safely. We have seven hours of darkness left; perhaps not even that. Realistically, we probably have six and half hours; we need to make the journey to the coast as speedily as possible."

Through the night the buses moved; it was almost unbelievable, but they were not challenged in any location. Even if they had known what had occurred on their soil, the collapsing infrastructure of each of the countries – especially Mozambique – together with the multitude of internal issues that the nations had been dealing with, had not left them with a defence force strong enough to respond.

At each of the Jihadi extremist camps, which had been in fairly remote locations, the local people would have seen the blasts and heard the gunfire. But for many of them there was a deep reluctance to move at night, never knowing what they would run into. Most of them would be waiting for the breaking of the dawn before they sought to alert any authorities.

The Special Force operators had also been very thorough in making sure that all the telephone lines were cut; any mobile phone towers within the immediate vicinity had been destroyed as well.

The planning had been meticulous; the implementation had been precise and professional. Just before dawn, the buses were rapidly closing on the coast of Mozambique – all except one. The troops from Zambia, despite having had a particularly high-speed journey through the dark night, were not going to make the sunrise deadline.

~~~~~

Close to the coast of Mozambique, a number of big yachts were anchored in various locations – two south of Nampula and four south of Quelimane, all anchored off the beach in deserted parts of the coastline. Further south, another four yachts were anchored between the Xai Xai district and Beira.

Just before the dawn broke, Stuart came up on his radio and said, "Roger. Please give me a status report."

As the radio came alive, the SAS group that had carried out the attack on Nampula said, "We have just made contact with the yacht, and we will be making our way to it soon."

"Roger that," said Hulk. "Well done."

A similar call came in from the group that had hit the Jihadi camp based in the Kruger National Park to the south of Punda Maria. The final call came in from the SAS group coming from Zambia.

"We have encountered some very bad terrain on the roads; the likelihood of us making the coast
~~~~~

by dawn is not very good," their commander reported.

"Roger that," said Stuart. "I suggest you find yourself some thick bush, preferably in an area you think is not populated, and lay up for the day."

The commander came back and said, "Sir, if you don't mind, we would like to keep travelling; visibility will be much better in the day. Dressed as we are, I think we may be able to bluff our way through."

Stuart came back on the radio and said, "Negative to that. Negative to that. I know Mozambique very well; and during the daylight, you will encounter multiple police roadblocks, not there to police you but looking for their bribes. It's just too dangerous; one of them may twig to you, and we'll end up with a firefight on our hands."

"Roger that, Hulk. I hadn't thought of that; thanks very much. Will do as you requested."

"Roger that," said Hulk. "The yacht will be lying off shore, the crew on board will be snorkelling and diving as though they are regular tourists. Rendezvous with them once darkness has fallen and you reach the coast."

"Roger that," came back the radio call.

Stuart turned to Tom and said, "This creates a slight issue for us in that we will be abandoning our buses very close to where the other pickup point is."

Stuart thought for a moment then came back up on the radio said, "Popeyes 5 and 6, do you copy?"

The radio came alive. "Popeyes 5 and 6 reading you fives; go ahead."

"Hulk here, Popeyes 5 and 6. I need you to up anchor and move north towards the new extraction point I will send you; I'm going to bring your group out further north than your current designated position. Our group will still make rendezvous with Popeyes 3 and 4 as planned."

"Roger that, Hulk. We copy," replied Popeyes 5 and 6.

Between Stuart and Popeyes 5 and 6, they quickly worked out a new extraction point. Stuart came up on the battle net and made contact with the group that had carried out the raid in Zambia. "Roger, these are your new extraction coordinates. Popeyes 5 and 6 will be moving offshore but will be waiting for you this evening."

"Roger that, Hulk. Thanks very much," replied the SAS Commander.

~~~~~

Half an hour from dawn Stuart stood upon the deck of Popeye 3 and looked back towards the coast. Inland, dancing flames consumed the vehicles that they had commandeered to get them to this point; the operators had been very thorough in setting fire to them using highly flammable incendiaries to set them alight. The Special Force operators needed to ensure that they left behind no DNA that could identify them and link them to the operation.
~~~~~

Popeyes 3 and 4 made their way out deeper into the Mozambique Channel, and once out of sight of the land made rendezvous with the British aircraft carrier that was on its normal patrol duties. As the different operators clambered aboard, making the transfer from the yachts, there was a great deal of banter and backslapping. They felt justifiably chuffed; this had been a clinical operation and to this point not a single soldier had become a casualty. Everything had gone like clockwork. Once they had dispatched their cargo of operators, the yachts continued on their logged courses as if they were just tourists cruising the Mozambique Channel.

Stuart moved down into the operations room, where he met with the captain of the aircraft carrier. Commodore Evans came up as he came in and shook his hand and said, "Well done, you guys; you did a tremendous job. We have been monitoring the civilian radio stations, and at this stage they are not reporting anything."

Stuart thought for a moment and said, "I doubt very much that the governments will be putting this out on their national networks. Remember, the presence of these extremist Jihadi training camps in the countries was not public knowledge. Remember, too, that all of these countries are receiving extensive aid from the West; the last thing that they want is to publicise the fact that these camps even existed. I don't believe we will hear anything on the public radio, but I think that our message would have gotten through very clearly.

Wherever these extremists are, wherever they seek to hide, whatever rock they find themselves under, we will find them. We will pursue them. And we will make them pay for every single life that they have taken."

Stuart's mind flashed back to that day, which seemed an age ago, when these Islamic extremists had launched the attacks on the ten towns of Cornwall. Stuart remembered the attack on Perranporth, the town that Stuart had lived in; remembered the attack that had involved him in foiling their plan and which had started this journey on which he now found himself. Pondering the thought that every single Jihadi extremist was covered in the blood of those innocent people, Stuart moved below decks to where his operators were gathering in the big conference room. Joining them he said, "Right, let's shut the door."

They shut the door, and Stuart turned and said, "Guys, we need to pray in absolute unity and give thanks to our Lord." Every single operator, male and female, bowed their heads as Stuart led them in a prayer of thanks, a simple warrior's prayer.

"Thank You, Lord, that today You went before us. Thank You, Lord, that today we were able to deal with an enemy that had taken a sworn oath to eradicate every single Christian believer, and anybody who supported the Western World. Thank You, Lord, that You have been our strength and our shield. We praise You and give You all the glory and all the honour and all the praise. Amen."

The aircraft carrier continued its northern cruise up the Mozambique Channel. Far to the south a Mayday call was put out by a yacht; the yacht was apparently experiencing difficulties. The aircraft carrier acknowledged the Mayday call and reversed its course, starting to make its way south in order to assist in the search for the yacht that appeared to be in trouble.

Of course there was no yacht in trouble; the Mayday call had been put out by Popeye 5 as a ruse to provide the aircraft carrier with a justifiable reason for turning round, bringing it closer to the Mozambique coast and positioning it in a viable place to make a pickup from Popeyes 5 and 6 once they had uplifted the troops who were still on the way.

It was a tense 24 hours, but eventually the call came through. Popeyes 5 and 6 had made their pickup of the designated Zambia-tasked operators; they were safely on board, and the yachts were now making their way speedily towards the aircraft carrier. Within a few short hours, the remainder of the operators who had carried out the four-fold operation into southern Africa, designated as "Operation Containment", were back on board the aircraft carrier. A short time later, a number of large transport planes arrived on the aircraft carrier; they left soon afterwards carrying the operators who had executed the successful mission.

Chapter Fifteen

Deep in a Jihadi training centre in Syria, Ishmael was sitting on his narrow, steel-framed bed, head bowed between his knees, sobs shaking his body. He had just heard the news of the total destruction of the four Jihadi Training Camps. What the Special Force operators could not have known was that leading each one of those camps was a son of Ishmael. Four sons, all camp commanders. Four sons, now dead.

One of those sons had been the young fanatic whom Bugs had observed through the eyes of his drone. That son had in fact been Ishmael's favourite.

For more than an hour, Ishmael sat on his bed sobbing. And then the tears dried. He stood and walked to the door of his hut and called out. Three other young men, the last of Ishmael's sons, made their way to the hut. He had had seven sons; the four eldest had died in the raids on the camps.

Ishmael turned to his remaining three sons and said, "I make an oath today, on your dead brothers' graves, that the man responsible for the death of your brothers, my sons, will pay! We will make him feel the pain that we have felt... and then, in the final moments, we will make him feel physical pain. Our mission right now is to find this man, to destroy him and his family, to destroy all hope of this unit of so-called Angels that he has created. He. Must. Die."

It was a glorious day. The sun was shining brightly. The sea was a wonderful blue. And all around the helipad, families – mothers, wives, husbands and children – were waiting as the big transport helicopters came in. Falling out of the sky like big fat geese, they discharged their load of happy passengers, men and women back from the frontlines of battle. The tarmac filled with men and women running across to greet husbands and wives and children; the sound of laughter floated across the area. The sound of happy children mingled with the tears of joy that so many of the wives were shedding.

Stuart and Tom were on board the last helicopter to come in. Stuart noticed that Tom was straining at the leash like a young hunting dog; he was so excited to be coming back to his family, to Trish and Sam. And he was really excited about the growing life that was within Trish. Stuart's eyes settled on his son, gratitude filling him. Tom had developed into an exceptional soldier who led his men with real maturity; he was a leader who genuinely cared for his soldiers, a leader who was prepared to and had put his life on the line, a leader who always led by example. Stuart looked up and silently prayed, "I want to thank You, Lord, for the wonderful children you have blessed me with."

As the helicopter touched down, Tom was the first one to leap off and run across the tarmac to his waiting wife and child. Stuart, with a bit more dignity as befitted his age, exited the helicopter – after all, while he was no longer the chubby gentleman he had once been, he was still a 55 year-old man. However, once he caught sight of Jane, he made his way smartly across the tarmac and gathered his wife into his arms, lifting her up off her feet and swinging her around. She giggled and said, "You had better be careful; just now you'll put your back out."

Stuart laughed, "You may well be right. They do say that you know you're getting old when your back goes out more than you do."

He gently put his treasured wife back on her feet, and then gathered her into his arms. As their lips met he again sent up a silent prayer thanking the Lord for giving him such a wonderful wife.

Once Stuart had collected his gear and slung it over his shoulder, he and Jane made their way down to the bungalow talking of the things that married couples often do, caught up and lost in themselves. Stuart had informed all the operators who had been on the mission that they would all have two weeks R&R to spend with their families. Unfortunately, because of his position and the situation at this moment in time, he wouldn't have that luxury.

~~~~~

Stuart was in early the next morning. As he made his way into his office, his daughter, Storm, popped her
~~~~~

head round the door and said, "Dad, call for you. It's the Prime Minister."

Stuart picked up the phone and said smartly, "Good morning, Mr Prime Minister. What can I do for you?"

The voice of David Cribbs came back. "First of all, Stuart, I'd like to congratulate you and all your men and women on the wonderful job that they've done. We are recommending that every single person who took part in the mission be granted the Military Cross."

Stuart smiled and said with a chuckle, "Thanks, David, that'll be good. A new one for my collection."

David's voice turned serious. "Stuart, I've got a huge favour to ask you." There was a pregnant silence, and then he continued, "As you know the general election is coming up in two months' time. The trouble is that our liberal coalition partners, whom we are hoping will not be part of the government after the election, are at the moment creating waves in the media.

"The Deputy Prime Minister has not forgiven you for the way that you embarrassed him in the Cobra meeting, and he has become very vocal in the press in the last week or so. He is claiming that your unit of Angels is in actual fact a modern day crusader outfit seeking to completely annihilate anybody who is not a Christian or sympathetic to Christians. You and I know that's not true, but that's the story he is putting out there... and it is gaining a lot of media attention. The favour I want to ask you, Stuart, is this: would you be prepared to go on national TV and refute these allegations and also very clearly inform the nation why you are doing what you are doing... and really just share the values that you hold to."

Stuart answered without a moment's hesitation. "Mr Prime Minister, it will be my pleasure."

The relief was evident in David Cribbs' voice. A strong liberal showing at the election in two months' time may well have forced the United Kingdom back into a coalition government, thereby weakening the nation substantially. "I'm so pleased to hear that, Stuart. I'll get my press secretary to set it up; it'll probably be with the BBC."

"Mr Prime Minister, whenever and with whomever, it's no problem; just let me know."

Two days later Stuart was waiting in the BBC green room, ready to go on the News Night programme that was going to air his interview. Stuart cut an impressive figure in full military uniform, his array of medals gleaming on his chest. If the liberals wanted a fight, he was more than up for it.

The BBC assistant came through and said, "Sir, they are ready for you now. Just a reminder that this will be going out live."

Stuart made his way across the stage as the host rose to his feet said, "Good evening, Sir. Welcome. Please take a seat."

Once they were comfortable, they got the call from the director, "Going live in 3, 2, 1..."

The camera swung to the host as he began his preamble. "Good evening. I am Jeremy Rink, and this is News Night. We are privileged this evening to have a very distinguished guest with us – the Duke of Perranporth, Field Marshal Stuart Flavell, the founder of the Special Assault Force, the hero of the Perranporth attack and the man who has been spearheading the different operations necessary to neutralise the Islamic threat."

Jeremy then turned to Stuart and said, "Thank you, Sir, for being with us."

Stuart's first comeback was, "Well, let's forget the sir; just call me Stuart."

Jeremy came back straightaway saying, "There is tremendous support for you within the nation; but, as you are aware, there is also an element within the nation that is accusing you of being a Christian crusader, of being a man who has created this unit with the specific purpose of annihilating Muslims. Stuart, what is your response to these allegations?"

Stuart leaned forward in his chair, his voice warm but firm, his eyes firmly engaged with the camera – he trusted firmly engaged with everybody who was watching this programme live – and said, "Jeremy, let me make it very clear that what we are about as a unit is not a crusade against the Islamic religion. Our mission, our goal is to protect the United Kingdom.

"My involvement began when the radicals, the extremist Jihadi warriors, attacked Perranporth. I was there and had past skills to prevent that massacre; from then on my involvement grew largely due to my past military experience... But now, before the nation, I want to make it absolutely crystal clear... I want to state unequivocally that the unit I lead, the men and woman I lead, are not Christian crusaders.

"Yes, we all believe in Jesus Christ as our personal Saviour. In fact, that is one of the stipulations that I put in place for the formation of that unit. This is because I have the firm belief that there is a spiritual dimension to the war we are waging.

"All over the world we see a rise in extremists, be they extremists from the extreme left..." Stuart paused to allow for a pregnant silence.

"... or from the extreme right. As a Christian I believe that God created every single man and every single woman. I also believe that one of the greatest gifts that God has given us as humankind is the gift of free choice; God doesn't force his will on anybody. I believe that He made the way for us to be forgiven of our sins and enjoy the redemptive life that we find in Jesus Christ.

"Through God's Son, Jesus Christ, and His finished work on the cross, we can find forgiveness when we come in faith and repentance. However, it is a matter of free choice; I *chose* to accept Jesus in faith and acknowledge my sin and repent of it. Nobody forced me to do that; that was *my free choice*. The Bible says very clearly that we are called not to judge, that the only One Who is in a position to judge is God Himself. The Bible also teaches that men and women will one day stand before God as individuals, and each one will be responsible for his or her own choice of whether to believe in Him or not.

"As a Christian I *must* respect the gift of free choice that God has given to every man and woman. If they choose to be Muslims, they have that right. If they choose to be Christians, they have that right. If they choose to follow some other religion or if they choose to follow no religion, that is their free choice.

"The force that I lead does not go out into the streets and threaten people with death if they do not believe what we believe. We do not go out into the streets and blow up people who hold a different view to us. We are soldiers who believe in democracy, who believe in the rule of law and the privilege of free speech. We believe in the right that each person has before God to believe what they choose to believe... Why? Because ultimately it will be that choice that they will have to stand by one day when God judges.

"So, Jeremy, we do not seek to enforce our will on anybody. However... the Muslim extremists, the Jihadi warriors we have been dealing with, do *not* hold to that same philosophy.

"They believe that everybody must believe what they believe; and if you don't believe what they believe, then you must die. They go out of their way to attack, slaughter and murder innocent men, women and children. They behead people, and that is a different issue altogether. *That* is a form of dictatorship! *That* is a form of fanaticism! The extreme Muslim Imams preach hatred, war and the eradication of all who do not believe as they do.

"That is *not* what we are about. My role, and the role of my unit, is to protect what is the inalienable right of every single man and woman in United Kingdom to believe what they believe in, freedom, to protect their right to speak out and share what they believe without fear of repercussion. *But* the moment they take that belief to an extreme view and use that extremist view to start hurting and killing people, then we will step in.

"I am a Christian, because I choose to be a Christian. I am a Christian, because I believe in God's Word, the Bible. I hold no personal opinions; my opinions as a servant of Jesus Christ are informed totally and solely by the Word of God. I don't get to pick and choose what parts of the Bible I will or won't believe. As a born-again believer, I have to accept *all* of God's Word, because it is *God's* Word... and it is what directs my life.

"Let me reiterate this. The Bible teaches very clearly that every single one of us will one day stand before God, and that every single one of us will give an account of the decisions we have made while we have been living on Earth. And therefore it is not my place to judge, but it is my place to respect everybody and their individual decisions about how they will live their lives and who they choose to believe in or not believe in. And therefore it is that freedom – that gift of free choice – that we protect.

"My men, my women, will go and die for those who today we are calling moderate Muslims, but are in fact not moderate Muslims; they are normal Muslims. They are men and women who believe in peace, who believe that their religion doesn't have to be a religion of violence and anger and slaughter. My men and women will protect them. My men and women will protect a Buddhist. My men and women will protect an atheist. Because my unit believes that we all have the freedom of choice! The fact that we as a unit have collectively chosen to believe in Jesus Christ as our personal Lord and Saviour does not change that belief; it is the very basis of that belief. We believe every time we go out to stand in the gap between the innocent people of this nation and this extremist onslaught that is coming our way, we are honouring God by being good citizens. Thank you."

Jeremy leaned back in his chair, clearly shocked by what Stuart had just said. It was obvious that he had been expecting a strong push for Christianity, yet the tables had been turned. And what he had heard was a man of integrity, who understood very clearly the teaching in the Bible that everybody had a free choice and that everybody would one day stand before God – Who Stuart personally knew beyond a shadow of a doubt would be Jesus Christ – and be judged.

Jeremy turned round to the cameras and said, "Well, ladies and gentlemen, there you have it; it is up to you to make up your minds. We would like to thank the Duke of Perranporth, Field Marshal Stuart Flavell, for taking time out of his very busy schedule to be with us. Thank you very much, and have a good evening."

~~~~~

The next day Stuart's interview was front-page news right across the whole nation. And 99% of the national newspapers had reported on it in a positive light, almost unheard of within the United Kingdom. But the UK was a nation that had been shocked, was a nation that had been alarmed at the degree of penetration the Muslim extremists had been able to achieve and the violence they had perpetrated on the nation that had fed and educated them. They had been kept up to date with press releases from David Cribbs' office, informing them exactly how serious the situation had been.

Stuart had not been back in his office very long when the telephone rang. It was the Prime Minister, David Cribbs. "Stuart, I want to thank you so much for what you said last night. My ratings are through the roof. And your popularity and the popularity of your unit is riding at an all-time high that has not been seen in this nation since Winston Churchill at the end of the Second World War."
~~~~~

He continued, "And I want to thank you personally, because what you said last night has helped me to clarify my own understanding of my stand before God and the fact that God has given me a free choice and that God will hold me responsible for my decision in regards to eternal things. It will be my decision and nobody else's by which I will stand.

"Stuart, I need to tell you that after watching you on TV last night, I got down on my knees in my office and gave my life to Jesus Christ. I thought I had been a Christian, but after what you said last night, I realised that I was only religious and had not really made that whole-hearted decision of my own free will, totally free from the politics of whether I followed or rejected Jesus Christ. I want you to know that I chose last night to follow Jesus Christ."

Stuart was thrilled to hear the news. "David, as a brother in the Lord, do you mind if I pray for you?"

Emotion carried in David Cribbs' voice as he came back and said, "Stuart, I would be honoured and blessed if you would pray for me."

Stuart prayed simply, "Dear Lord, please be with our Prime Minister... please be with David, as he leads this nation; help him to hear Your spirit, and help him to lead us with wisdom, integrity and courage in the run-up to the elections in the coming months. Lord, be his strength and his shield; protect him from being sucked into the sparring and the paper promises that form such a large part of an election year. Lord, rather let him speak the truth with integrity and honesty and trust this nation to do the right thing. Amen."

Stuart spoke to David then. "Welcome to the family, David. I know God is going to lead you in the months ahead." He went on to ask, "Mr Prime Minister, what about the liberal camp? What's their reaction to the media coverage? "

David chuckled on the other end of the phone. "Your interview last night has completely blown their smear campaign right out of the water; if they win one seat in Parliament, it will be a lot. I think that we will win a clear majority and be able to begin to ensure that this nation returns to its Christian roots, to the clear teachings from the Word of God that once made this nation great... before the modern church compromised and abandoned them while trying to be politically correct. Thank you so much! Have a good day."

CHAPTER SIXTEEN

Special Assault Force Base, Cornwall
Six weeks after the Southern African Operation

Down in the family bungalow section of the camp, Trish was feeling caged in. The growing life within had her hormones jumping, causing her emotions to oscillate all over the place. Tom was out on a training mission, and she and her sister, Lauren, were stuck in the camp. She craved the freedom to act on impulse, to go out and do something crazy.

The reality of their security status meant that even a trip to the shops meant a security detail had to tag along, and shopping trips had to be booked in advance. The normally level-headed Trish felt the seed of rebellion rising within her; she had a strong desire to go and shop for items for the baby's room. The fact that the birth of the baby was still six months away did not really impinge on her thoughts; the nesting syndrome that was kicking in was driving her. She just wanted to be out in Truro buying some babies clothes and showing her sister the sights.

Trish hesitated for a moment. She had promised this morning to look after Storm's daughter, Michelle. She thought for a moment, and then decided she would take Michelle along too; she loved to shop, especially if it was for the baby.

Ever since the Perranporth attacks and the start of Tom's involvement within the Special Assault

Force, things like a simple shopping trip had almost become like a military operation. Given the high profile of the unit and the fact that they were all targets for the Jihadi warriors, it was now standard protocol to have security go with them whenever they left the base. Today, Trish was feeling resentful that life was no longer simple. A little smile slipped onto Trish's face; just once they would escape for the day. Some shopping in Truro, followed by lunch and a stroll on the beach, sounded like heaven to her.

Trish called to her sister, Lauren, and said, "Come on, Lauren; were' going shopping."

Lauren looked at her sister with a questioning look in her eye and said, "But, Trish, aren't we supposed to go with an escort?"

"Not today. Today, we go on our own – you, me and Michelle. It's been six weeks since the operation, and things have been really quiet. I think the threat has pretty much disappeared for a while. And I really feel the need to go and do some shopping and get some stuff for the nursery. I've only got boy things left over from Sam, and this little girl growing in my womb feels the need for some girl things today."

Lauren smiled and said, "You're quite convinced it's a little girl?"

Trish nodded her head. "Yes, I know it's a little girl. I can just feel it; it's definitely going to be a little girl."

Twenty minutes later they drove up to the exit gate of the camp; the non-commissioned officer on duty came out and Trish said, "I'm just going into Truro on a quick shopping expedition."

The NCO looked at her quizzically and said, "Without your escort?"

Trish panicked for a moment, then said, "Don't worry; I cleared it with my husband."

The NCO knew that Trish's husband, Tom, was the commander of the Angels; he looked indecisive for a moment not sure whether to call out the wife of the commanding officer to find out whether she was telling the truth or not. He wrestled with his conflicting thoughts for a few moments and then gave the signal to the guardroom to raise the boom of the gate.

Trish accelerated quickly through the great gate, a feeling of exultation sweeping through her. The rapidly changing hormones within her body blinded her completely to the danger that she had placed them in. Danger was the last thing on their minds as they sped down the road, wind blowing in their hair and the fresh sea air invigorating them. Within twenty minutes the car full of happy ladies and one very excited young girl arrived in Truro. Trish parked the car, and they set off on an extensive shopping spree moving from baby shop to baby shop.

~~~~~

Back at the SAF base, Storm, on her tea break, made her way up to Trish's bungalow. Storm
~~~~~

knocked on the door and got no answer. Thinking it strange, she knocked again; still no answer came. Turning the handle, she walked in through the unlocked door calling out as she went. No response.

She called again, "Trish? Lauren? Michelle?" Still no answer.

Storm pulled out her mobile and phoned Jane, "Hi, Mom. Are Trish, Lauren and Michelle with you?"

"Hi, Storm. No, they're not here. I'm down on the base beach spending a little one on one time with Sam... Why? What's wrong?"

"I'm at their bungalow now, and there is no sign of them. They never called for an escort, though, so they couldn't have left the base. Thanks, Mom. Talk later."

Despite her calm words, Storm felt a rising sense of panic; something was not right. Moving across to the internal base telephone, she picked it up and called the guardroom. When the duty NCO answered she said, "Hello. This is Captain Storm Ireland. Has my sister-in-law, Trish Flavell, gone out at all?"

The NCO came back quickly and said, "Yes Ma'am. She left about twenty minutes ago, together with her sister and your daughter."

Storm felt the panic rising. "Did they have an escort with them?"

"No, Ma'am," came the answer. "Mrs Flavell said she had cleared it with her husband and that all was okay for her to go without escorts."

Storm thanked the NCO and cut the connection. She immediately dialled the operations room; the operator answered on the first ring. Storm said, "Please find the Hulk and patch him through to me; we have a situation that has developed."

Within seconds Stuart came on to the line, "Hi, Storm. What's up, honey?"

"Dad, we have a situation. Trish and Lauren have gone shopping in Truro; they have taken Michelle with them... and they didn't arrange for an escort."

There was just a moment's silence, and then Stuart responded, "Okay, get back to the operations room and activate *Operation Bloodhound*."

Operation Bloodhound was a tracking system the unit had decided upon as an extra layer of security. Each person that was on the base had a tracker chip that linked to GPS; it would be in their handbag, on some part of the body in a watch or bracelet, or wherever they felt comfortable having it. Storm ran down to the operations room where she activated Operation Bloodhound. She rapidly put in the identity codes for Trish and Michelle; as a visiting guest, Lauren didn't have a tracker. Within a short space of time, their location was up on the screen.

Storm came back up on the battle net. "Hulk, Hulk, do you copy?"

Hulk came back straight away and said, "Roger, Countess. Copy."

"Dad, it looks like they are in or close to Mothers' Planet in Truro at the moment."

"Roger. Copy that, Countess. Bugs and I are downtown at the moment; we were doing surveillance training in Truro with some of the other operators. We'll move in and see if we can secure them," replied Stuart.

"Roger that; please keep me informed," Storm said with an edge of desperation in her voice.

Within seconds, Stuart, Bugs and three other operators were making their way up the cobbled street towards Mothers' Planet in Truro. They were about 400 metres away when, suddenly, there was a burst of gunfire; screams began to erupt all along the street, as people looked for cover or just stood around in absolute confusion not sure what was happening.

As Hulk, Bugs and the other operators – now at full sprint – neared Mothers' Planet, they saw four men exit the shop. In the arms of the man in the lead was young Michelle, Stuart's granddaughter. Waiting right outside the door was a minivan. The man carrying Michelle dived through its open door, closely followed by two of the other men – one young and one about Stuart's age. The man in the rear was carrying an AK-47 and firing random shots into the air.

Stuart slid to a stop and squeezed off two rounds from his Sig Sauer P239-9mm; the erratic shooter slumped to the ground. The door of the minivan slammed shut, and the minivan took off at high speed.

Stuart sprinted up to the now still body lying on the cobblestones, a widening pool of blood rapidly spreading around him. As Stuart looked down, he knew for sure that this young man was dead; two bullets had taken him cleanly in the head. Bugs meanwhile had leapfrogged past Stuart and sprinted into Mothers' Planet, closely followed by the other operators.

As he entered the store, he saw a group of people kneeling by two women; both of their chests were covered in blood. The first woman was Trish, she had taken two hits in the chest, and the red bloodstain was rapidly spreading across her chest. Lying not far from her was her sister, Lauren, also with a reddening pool of blood spreading across her right chest and shoulder. Bugs leapt forward and shouted into his radio, "We need a medevac at Mothers' Planet, Truro. Dude's wife is down; Dude's sister-in-law is down. Both critical. We need a medevac stat!"

Back in the operations room, Storm heard Bugs' words and a cold dread seeped through her. She could not move; her body seemed to turn to jelly as a cold wave of absolute dread washed over her. Forcing herself to act, she came back on the radio and said, "Michelle... What about Michelle?"

At that point the Stuart broke onto the battle net and said, "Countess, this is Hulk. We have a white minivan, registration Whiskey X-Ray 60 Papa Uniform Lima, moving out of Truro... last seen heading up the hill towards the Newquay road. If they are sighted proceed with care. They've got Michelle. She is alive, but they are armed and very dangerous.”

Those were the last words Storm heard, as she collapsed onto the operation room floor in a dead faint.

Meanwhile Major Franks, aka Bugs, had dropped to his knees next to Trish; she was still breathing. Grabbing some white T-shirts off the rack at Mothers’ Planet, he made a pressure bandage and pushed it down onto the wounds in Trish’s chest; one of the other operators was bending over Lauren doing exactly the same thing, trying to stem the flow of blood. Stuart came into the store, took in the scene at a glance and came up on the battle net. “Angels Roost, do you copy? This is Hulk.”

The ops room came up straightaway. “Roger, Hulk. We copy. Go.”

Stuart said, “I want a general alert. I want all Angels mobilised and ready to go. Get hold of Dude and get him down to the Royal Cornwall Hospital ASAP; his wife has been critically injured, as has her sister, Lauren.”

“Roger that, Hulk,” confirmed the operations room.

Within seconds the call was going out to all the different Angel units, and the personnel promptly began to make their way to their operational stations kitting up into full battledress.

The medevac helicopter, which was always on standby at the special force base, was already in the air. Within minutes, it was over Truro and came into land just a few hundred metres away from Mothers' Planet. The doctor and medics were out in a flash, running down to Mothers' Planet, assessing the situation, getting drips into Trish and Lauren, lifting them onto stretchers and then into the helicopter. The helicopter rose and began the short journey to the Royal Cornwall Hospital, already alerted to receive incoming casualties.

The radio crackled, "Hulk, Hulk, this is Angels Roost. Do you copy?"

"Roger. Go," said Hulk.

The operations room reported, "We just had news; the police found the white van abandoned not far outside of Truro. It looks like they switched vehicles, so at this stage we don't know what vehicle they're driving... Hulk, they did find an envelope in the vehicle... addressed to you. The police have opened it, and it is a threat. It says that they are going to destroy you, the unit and your family. The note also says that it will be your personal Trafalgar and that they will strike a blow, which will rock this nation and its heroes."

"Say again," said Hulk. "Did the note specifically say it would be my personal Trafalgar?"

"Affirmative to your query, Hulk," came back Angels Roost.

"Roger that. Do you have anything on the tracker that we had on Michelle; it was in her headband?"

"Negative to that; her tracking device still shows her to be in Mothers' Planet."

"Roger that," said Stuart. "I want Angels 1 mobilised. I want them to get up to London, and I want them to do a full assessment of Trafalgar Square. I want a full security matrix and scenario solutions. I think there was a clue in that note; whoever these people are, they are planning to strike. And they want to draw us into Trafalgar Square. I think that's where they're planning the next operation, and they're not scared. They want us to be there. This is a personal revenge attack, and they need to draw us out. Let's look for fingerprints on the hostile that we took down; perhaps they will give us some clue as to whom we are dealing with here. Roger. Hulk out."

Stuart swung round and said to Bugs, "Bugs, I want you to mobilise *Operation Deep Diver*. We need to find Michelle."

"Roger that, Hulk," said Bugs, pulling an electronic tablet from his inside pocket. Bugs punched in some codes and then said to Stuart, "Deep Diver is activated and tracking."

Only Stuart and Bugs knew of Operation Deep Diver. Working unbeknown to any members of his family, Stuart had had a microchip half the size of a grain of sand implanted under the scalp of each one of his grandchildren. This was an experimental project; it was also very scary and controversial to any Christian. The microchip Stuart had implanted only gave the identity and location of the person it was implanted into; however, it did bear some similarities to the mark of the beast that the Bible spoke about, the mark which many Christians believed would be a microchip carrying all their personal and banking information and which could also allow the person to be tracked. No Christian would ever accept that microchip, which the Bible said would be implanted either on the hand or on the forehead. Stuart himself would never accept that type of chip. As a Christian, he could not.

However, the experimental chips that he had used on his grandchildren were implanted behind the ear and only gave identity and location. If the experiment worked, the plan was for all members of the unit to carry this basic type of identification and geo information to assist with rescue and identification.

"Right, Bugs. What is the chip telling us regarding Michelle's whereabouts?" asked Stuart.

"Hulk, the chip is feeding back to us that Michelle is heading up towards London at a speed of 250 kilometres per hour and is at an altitude of 10,000 metres. She must be in some sort of aircraft, possibly a private plane," said Bugs.

"Okay, let's keep monitoring her. I suspect they won't harm her yet; they need her alive to carry out what I believe is their plan of revenge against us and the nation."

At this point one of the operators who had been with Stuart and Bugs approached. "We have the statements taken from those who were in the store when the attack happened; they tell a very simple story. Trish, Lauren and Michelle were looking at baby clothes when four men with very dark complexions walked in wearing long jackets. One of the men opened his jacket, pulled out a sub-machine gun, and shot Trish and Lauren; then, the older one of the four grabbed Michelle, and they exited the store. Clean, concise and clinical. They knew exactly who they were after, which means they must have been watching the base for a long time – just waiting for an opportunity."

"Right," said Stuart. "We can make our way back to base now."

~~~~~

By the time Stuart and Bugs arrived back at base, the reports were flooding in. The doctors were working on Trish. The hospital reported she had sustained two gunshot wounds to the chest; fortunately both of them were high on the left-hand side and had not hit any vital organs. The vital signs of the baby that she was carrying were still strong, and the medics were confident that she would pull through. Lauren had also sustained a gunshot wound high into the right shoulder, but her prognosis was good. One thing was sure: the gunman was not the best of shots, a fact the Flavell and Ireland families were very grateful for. The now-dead gunman had fired quickly and randomly and had failed to ensure that his shots had indeed killed the intended victims.
~~~~~

By this time Tom, who had been on a field exercise with some of his operators, was making his way by helicopter to the Royal Cornwall Hospital. As he sat in the helicopter, the stress and pain was chiselled on his face as various thoughts ran through his mind. What had happened? Was his wife alive or ...? Tom thought of his son; Sam had been spending the day down on the beach below with his Granny Jane. Would he now be left without a mommy? What about the unborn child that was growing in Trish's womb?

As the fear, anguish, pain and anger, a negative cocktail of emotions that was testing Tom's faith, surged through his mind, he took a deep breath and bowed his head and said, "Lord, I need You to be my strength and my shield at this moment in time. Please calm me down. I pray... I pray that You would be with Trish. I pray that You would be with Lauren. And, Lord, I pray that You would be with Michelle; keep Your hand upon her and keep her safe as well." As Tom prayed these words, tears rolling down his cheeks, the operators around him in the helicopter bowed their heads and prayed for their commanding officer as he dealt with the personal pain and anguish of the situation that had arisen.

As the helicopter touched down at the Royal Cornwall Hospital, Tom exited like a speeding bullet and quickly made his way into the hospital. He was greeted there by the medical staff who gave him the reassuring news that, although Trish had sustained two very serious wounds to the left-hand upper chest, none of them had hit the vital organs and she was expected to make a full recovery. The baby, too, seemed unaffected. Likewise, Lauren, who'd had a much lesser injury, would also make a full recovery.

As he made his way into the room where Trish was, Tom sent up a silent prayer of praise and thanks to the Lord for the fact that He had spared his wife and sister-in-law. Trish was still heavily sedated, fast asleep and pale as a ghost. Tom took her hand in his and simply relished the feel of living flesh between his hands.

Minutes later, Stuart walked into the room, came across to Tom, put his arm around his son's shoulder and said, "Tom, I am so glad that Trish and Lauren will be alright. I have arranged to have their parents flown out from South Africa; they need to be here with their daughters as well."

Tom looked into his dad's eyes, the tears in his own eyes mirrored in Stuart's, and said, "Dad, what about Michelle? How are Storm and Steve coping?"

"I won't lie to you, Tom; they are in a bad way. Storm collapsed when she heard the news, and Steve is like a raging bull," said Stuart. "I know where they are taking Michelle, though." Stuart quickly filled Tom in on the note that had been left in the van. "I have no doubt that this is a revenge attack, that these men have deliberately targeted our family because of our involvement in this unit. This is more than just an Islamic extremist Strike. For some reason, somehow, this has become personal for them.”

The words were hardly out of Stuart's mouth, when his radio earpiece came alive as a report came through. Stuart nodded a few times then said, “Roger that.” Stuart turned round to Tom and said, “Well, we now have positive confirmation. They checked the fingerprints of the hostile that we shot in Truro. It turns out that he is known, and was last heard of in Syria. His name was Husain; and he was the son of Ishmael, the man who was the Imam of the Sono Mosque. He was the one who seemed to have escaped from the extremist ship we seized off McRae Island. You will remember that he was the planner and controller of the group that infiltrated the SAS.”

Tom nodded his head. “So, it was personal...” At that moment Trish groggily began to open her eyes. As she came to full wakefulness and Tom's face swam into focus, the first words that left her lips were, “Tom, I'm so sorry. I'm so sorry. I know I should not have gone. I'm so sorry! Are Lauren and Michelle alright?”

Tom hesitated before he answered. “Lauren was wounded but should be okay. But unfortunately, Trish... they kidnapped Michelle.”

Trish's face paled even more; tears welled up in her eyes and then spilled over her eyelids to stream down her cheeks. She love her little niece so much, and now her few moments of rebellion had resulted in Michelle’s life being put in danger. “Tom,

I'm just so sorry. I'm *so* sorry. I don't know what came over me; I just felt like I had to get out. I just felt I needed to get things ready in the nursery. I wasn't thinking straight."

Tom reached across and grabbed her hand and said, "Honey, I understand; sometimes when you're pregnant, the hormones can scramble things up a little bit. We will do our best to get Michelle back alive, but you need to know that Storm and Steve are taking it really badly. We need to pray for them. And what *you* need to do at the moment is focus on getting better."

Stuart reached down to touch Trish's hand and said, "We will be bringing Lauren into your room soon to keep you company; Tom will be here with you." Stuart saw a look of protest begin to form on Tom's face, looked him in the eye and said, "Tom, I am standing you down from this operation; you need to be here with your wife and family. You need to be focused in our type of work. In an operation when you are worrying about Trish, you may miss a vital clue. Plus, we need some sort of security around here; the local news has already reported on the attack and the fact that neither Trish nor Lauren were actually killed. We don't know that these guys will not try again. I need you here to protect them; is that understood?"

Tom understood very clearly. This wasn't his dad, Stuart, speaking; this was a direct order coming from Field Marshal Flavell, the supreme commander of the Special Forces. Tom looked up, his shoulders squared, "Yes, Sir, clearly understood."

"Right then," said Stuart. Bending down and giving Trish a quick kiss on her forehead, he said, "You had better get well, my girl. Now look after that little baby growing inside of you. And pray for us; we have work to do." With those words Stuart exited the hospital room, making his way to a waiting helicopter. They lifted off and soon arrived back at the base.

Stuart was greeted with the sight of his wife, Jane, and little Sam standing at the helipad. Stuart climbed out of the helicopter, made his way across to Jane, put his arm around her and Sam and said, "Trish and Lauren are going to be okay. Tom's with them now."

Jane said, "We need to go see our daughter. Storm's taking Michelle's kidnapping very badly, and Steve is beside himself."

Stuart and Jane, together with little Sam, made their way across to Storm's bungalow, and without the courtesy of knocking made their way through the door which was standing open. Their daughter, Storm, was sitting on the sofa. It was clear she had been through literal hell on earth in the last few hours. As a mother she had to try and come to terms with the knowledge that her daughter was in the hands of Jihadi extremists, and the thought of their six-year-old daughter in their hands was driving her crazy.

Steve was a mixture of emotions. He wavered between fear and anger and pain. He was torn between the desire for revenge and a feeling of helplessness.

Stuart came across to them, got down on his knees and took Storm's hands in his. Jane sat next to Storm and put her arms around her daughter. Stuart said, "I am confident that I know where they are taking Michelle. I've mobilised Angels 1, and they are already making their way up to London. This was a personal attack on us as a family, and I am so sorry that you have been drawn into it too.

"I'm making my way up to London within the next twenty minutes. Storm, I'm standing you down; Steve, you need to be with your wife and support her. Jane, you need to be here, covering us all with your prayers. We need God's help and wisdom."

Stuart looked up at his daughter, and with tears rolling down his face said, "Know this Storm: I will do everything I can before God to get Michelle back alive. What I need now is for you, Steve and Mom to be praying like you've never prayed before. We are in a huge spiritual battle, and we need those prayers. Storm, we need you to pray!"

Storm's eyes cleared and she said, "Thank you, Dad. We will be praying like we've never prayed before." As she finished speaking, she broke into a fresh bout of crying, the sobs coming from her chest with real pain. Stuart walked out of the bungalow, the sounds of her tears and pain echoing in his ears.

A deep sorrow and pain washed over Stuart, and as he made his way down to the helipad, he quietly asked, "Lord, why do we have so much pain?"

The answer flashed back. "You don't have to carry this pain; remember, I paid the price and carried your pain for you. Just trust me."

Stuart felt a great peace come over him. He knew God was in control. He knew that his physical Angels were moving into position around Trafalgar Square in London; and he now knew that the spiritual Angels of the Living God were all around them, contending in the spiritual realm for them. Stuart was conscious that this was a spiritual battle between the forces of evil, seeking to subvert all that is good and pure, and the army of the Most High God. With those thoughts on his mind, Stuart climbed aboard the helicopter, which was soon winging its way up country towards London.

~~~~~

Trafalgar Square, London
11:00hours the next day

It was a glorious day in London. The city was teeming with people – locals and tourists, men, women and children – some making their way to work, others stopping to enjoy the sights in the sunshine or ride the open-top tour buses.

Stuart sat at the side of Trafalgar square, looking at home on the steps that led up to the
~~~~~

National Gallery. He spoke into his radio, "What's the status of Michelle's Deep Diver tracker?"

Bug's came back straight away; he was monitoring the chip from the Royal Cornwall Hospital where he and Tom were following the goings on in London, while at the same time keeping an eye on the ladies. "Roger, Hulk," he said. "I can confirm they are there. You should be able to see them making their way from the east side of the square towards the centre."

Stuart lifted his eyes, and sure enough, he could see a man with the young girl in a red coat – Michelle's favourite coat, given to her by Granny and Grandpa – making their way towards the square. His heart racing, Stuart said, "All Angels, listen. I am pretty sure they have put a suicide vest on her; I want the mobile phone blocking protocol activated immediately."

This was new technology that the Angels were using. They were able to block the mobile phone signals in an area up to a three mile radius. Stuart was convinced that these Islamic extremists would not activate the bomb themselves; that because this was a personal revenge attack, they had to draw the Angels in while leaving themselves an exit route. By leaving Michelle with a suicide vest in Trafalgar Square, they probably hoped all the Angels moving in to secure her, as well as the mass of civilians in the area, would be caught in the blast after they detonated the vest remotely. It would create a major incident that would bring fear into the hearts of so many people and destroy much of the unit that had foiled so many of their plans.

Stuart looked out across the square and said, "Yes, I see them. The older man is moving away. Keep eyes on him. Don't let him slip the net. I'm going to Michelle; she needs to see her grandpa. She will talk to me and give us the answers we need regarding what she is wearing. I want the Holdfast Angels to converge on me and Michelle ASAP." The Holdfast Angels were the engineers, the men and women trained to deal with just such a situation as they now found themselves in.

As about twenty different Angels began to converge on Michelle, the dark-skinned, older man began to withdraw faster, making his way toward the exit by the Fourth Plinth. It was Ishmael. With a smile like a rabid wolf on his face, he quickly made his way through the throng of people. Soon, he would have his revenge. Soon, this infidel dog that had plagued him would die. He was convinced the man would be there to rescue his granddaughter; this was his chance.

On one point Ishmael was not wrong. Stuart was the first to reach Michelle; the little girl's eyes turned to her grandpa, fear and the anguish written in them. Stuart said, "Michelle Honey, I want you to stand very still. Tell me; did those bad men put something on you?"

Michelle was a clever little girl, and even though she was feeling scared and traumatised, she nodded her head and said, "Yes, Grandpa. They put a very heavy jacket on me... and it hurts. I feel like I just want to sit down; it's very, very heavy."

"Okay, Love. We'll take care of it for you," said Stuart.

By this time Ishmael was almost running to get clear of the square. Once he had, once he felt he was far enough away, he turned and looked back. Sure enough, he could see a group of at least twenty different people in black combat gear around the little girl. And just as he had hoped, he saw an older man in civilian clothes; the man was down on his knees talking to the little girl. Ishmael pulled a pair of opera glasses out of his top pocket and focused them. For the first time he got a look at the face of the man who had been his nemesis, the man who – though Ishmael did not know it – had been led by God to block every single one of his plans. Stuart's face jumped sharply into focus, and Ishmael took perverse pleasure in seeing the pain etched on Stuart's face. With a feeling of absolute satisfaction, Ishmael pulled out his mobile phone and dialled the number of the handset attached to the suicide vest. When the mobile rang, it would activate the detonator and the vest would explode. Ishmael's revenge would be complete.

He dialled the number, pushed the call button and waited for the explosion. Nothing happened.

Ishmael looked at his mobile phone in more detail. It was showing no signal. That was impossible! The signal in Trafalgar Square was one of the best signals in England. He moved around and tried again and again. Still no signal!

Suddenly, the penny dropped. They had jammed all mobile signals. He swung round again and focused the opera glasses on the group. He could see that they had removed the little girl's coat and that at least another hundred soldiers, dressed in black fatigues, had moved in and were starting to move people away from the little girl. He could see that some of the men were down on their knees working on the little girl, and he felt a sense of total frustration. This was a very primitive suicide vest; they hadn't had time to get a very sophisticated one, which had anti-bomb disposal booby-traps built into it. There were only two ways of detonating's this vest – manually or remotely via the mobile phone. And Ishmael knew there was now no way for him to get back to the little girl to detonate the vest manually. There were just too many soldiers in the square forming a ring of steel around her.

Deep anger at being thwarted once again welled up within Ishmael, and a dark form seemed to come over his face. Anybody looking at his face in that moment in time would have seen what almost appeared to be a mask of the son of perdition, the son of darkness, the devil himself.

Distracted by the immense ire raging within him, Ishmael had missed a vital clue on his last look through the opera glasses. Stuart was no longer in the square.

As Ishmael made his exit down Whitcomb Street, frustration and anger boiling within him, he heard a voice call out his name.

"Ishmael, Ishmael."

Ishmael swung around. There, standing before him, was the older man that he had seen in the square. Ishmael felt a sense of panic rising within him; never before had he seen eyes that so blazed with fury, yet at the same time seemed ice cold. The eyes were so cold that he felt like the hand of death itself had reached out and touched him. Breaking his gaze from those frightening eyes, Ishmael's hand dived into his jacket pocket. Screaming in hate and anger, spit flying from his lips, Ishmael dragged his gun clear and started to bring it up. He would kill this infidel dog.

As Ishmael's gun came clear, Stuart's hand rose with absolute precision; and with the coldness of the professional soldier that he was, he fired two quick shots, both of them striking Ishmael in the head and bringing down the man who had been the mastermind behind the plan to wreak havoc in the UK. Ishmael had planned the deaths of so many innocent people; he had led so many young people astray. But in that flickering moment, his life was extinguished. Job done.

Stuart moved forward and stood over the now lifeless body. He knew in his heart of hearts that Ishmael would now receive his true judgement, as he stood before the King of Kings and Lord of Lords. He also knew that he had carried out his duty, both as a protector of his own family, and also of his unit and the nation as well. Stuart spoke into his radio, sending the message across the battle net. "I need a containment team at my location in Whitcomb Street. The team will need a body bag and forensics kit."

As Stuart made his way back to the square after the arrival of the containment team, he was brought up to date by his on-site intel officer who reported, "I suspect the hostile you neutralized was Ishmael; he was the leader of the group. The intel we gleaned from Michelle as the engineers were working on her suggests that were four men in the van with her. We believe two of them were Ishmael's sons, another one a cousin and, of course, the last was Ishmael himself. That leaves three hostiles still unaccounted for."

~~~~~

From the other side of Trafalgar Square, Ishmael's son, Omar, and his cousin, Hussain, had observed what had happened. They did not know that Ishmael was dead; they had lost sight of him. But they realised the plan had failed. The suicide vest was now off the little girl, and an older man was making his way across the square. Once he reached her, he lifted her into his arms and hugged her. With the immediate danger contained, the soldiers were starting to expand their containment cordon. Omar and Hussain joined the crowd and moved away from
~~~~~

the scene. Their objective was to get to a safe house, wait for Ishmael and then find out what he wanted them to do.

By the time they arrived back at their safe house, the BBC was already giving in-depth coverage of the incident and acknowledging that one of the terrorists had been killed. He was identified as Ishmael Bin Quin, the former Imam at the Sono Mosque in South London, and a wanted man. Omar and Hussain struggled to come to terms with the news of Ishmael's death and the fact that they had failed again; they couldn't understand it. But they knew that another opportunity would one day present itself, and they would eventually be able to strike a mortal blow.

~~~~~

Royal Cornwall Hospital, Truro, Cornwall

Tom was semi-asleep on the chair next to his wife's bedside, when he became conscious that there was somebody else in the room. Tom looked up and saw a doctor dressed in a white lab coat, pushing a dressing trolley with a green material cover over it. As Tom's eyes cleared, he looked up at the man's face; what he saw there sent him into instant action. He exited his chair in a rolling dive, rolled onto the floor and in one smooth move drew his P239-9mm. Simultaneously, the man in the lab coat tore back the green cloth on the dressing trolley. Beneath the cloth
~~~~~

was an AKM folding butt rifle, a deadly weapon that the man was now lifting and swinging up towards Tom. There was a look of complete hatred on his face, his dark complexion and facial features giving testimony to his Arab linage. This was Abdul, one of Ishmael's remaining sons; he had returned to complete the job that they had failed to do in Mothers' Planet in Truro.

As Tom finished rolling, Abdul was already aligning the AKM for a shot. But Tom's training and instincts were just that much better, that much faster; his P239-9mm barked twice, followed by another two shots. The attackers' head exploded back — two bullets in his head, two bullets in his chest. As he crashed to the floor, the sound of the AKM-47 falling combined with the shots that had rung out brought Trish and Lauren to alarmed wakefulness. The sounds also brought Bugs, who had been out in the corridor speaking to one of the nurses, running through the door. The scene before him told its own story to a trained soldier.

Tom walked across and looked down at the dead man, who now lay on the floor. He felt no sadness in his heart, just a quiet calm that another one of those who had sought to bring pain and death to the innocent had been dealt with. Tom turned and made his way across to his wife. Trish and Lauren were sitting up, their eyes as huge as saucers, shaking in reaction as adrenaline slowed. Tom put his arms around Trish and said, "Don't worry, Love. It's all okay now."

Lauren, in the bed next to her, broke down into tears; and Bugs, who was standing in the doorway, felt this sudden compulsion to go across and comfort her. Bugs was not married. Yet he hardly knew Lauren, had maybe spoken a few words in greeting when first meeting her. But suddenly, he felt that he had to go across and comfort her. Almost of their own volition, his feet started moving in her direction. Lauren looked up through the curtain of tears pouring down her face to see the handsome young man standing next to her. "Don't worry, Lauren; it's alright. Tom has taken care of the danger."

As Bugs reached out and touched her shoulder, Lauren felt as though a jolt of electricity had jumped from the man's hand. It was almost like he was soldering together an emotional circuit; a sense of completeness and total peace came over her. With shy, tear-stained eyes, she glanced up at him, a red blush staining her cheeks and a breathlessness gathering in her chest; he was rather handsome. Lauren noticed that Bugs also seemed to think something very significant had just happened.

Bugs was feeling bemused. He too had felt that same jolt of electricity, something he had never experienced before; and he looked at Lauren with a sense of wonderment and confusion. He had not noticed at their brief meeting just how beautiful she actually was. Bugs was jolted from his feeling of wonder as Tom's voice broke into his daydream.

"We should get a containment clean-up team in here. You had better believe that this will be all over the news in no time." Tom gestured to the gathering nursing staff outside the doors, some of them already reporting the news on Social Media.

<center>~~~~~</center>

Two hours later a helicopter touched down on the helipad at the special force base in Cornwall. As the door slid back, a little girl in a red coat – a little girl full of energy and life – exploded from the helicopter and tore across the helipad, literally launching herself into the arms of Mommy and Daddy who were standing to the side of the landing area. Steve and Storm were certainly blown away by how God had preserved their daughter. The little family got down on their haunches, hugging, crying and laughing together, united once again.

Stuart climbed out of the helicopter, looked across at his daughter and her little family, and again sent up a prayer of thanks to God for His hand of keeping that had once again protected them through all the tears and pain.

Michelle chattered away, eager to tell her parents about all of her experiences, proving the remarkable resilience that children have even in traumatic times. Storm gathered Steve and Michelle close and said, "I have something to tell you."

Something in the tone of Storm's voice dried up Michelle's flow of words, and a look of puzzlement formed on her young face. Steve also looked bemused. Storm gathered them even closer and, giving them each a big kiss, said, "Mommy's pregnant; you're going to have a little brother."

Michelle's' face broke out into absolute joy and excitement; the experiences of the past few days were forgotten, the idea of a new little brother washing them from her mind. Michelle laughed as the little family stood up and began to make their way down towards their bungalow. Storm paused and looked back over her shoulder, her eyes meeting those of her dad who was following behind. Her lips mouthed a silent 'thank you' as the tears of joy began again. Stuart nodded, his own eyes filling with tears of joy.

As they walked, Steve felt completely astounded, but also excited at the news that soon their little family of three would become four. He too sent up a silent prayer of thanks to God for His hand of blessing and shield of protection that had been around Michelle.

~~~~

Special Assault Force Base, Cornwall
Two weeks later

Stuart and Jane stood on the cliffs overlooking the base beach, the brisk invigorating breeze whipping their hair. Stuart gathered Jane closer into his side and said, "Let's walk."

Hand in hand they walked along the cliffs, stopping at the two newly-erected memorials of
~~~~

black granite. One was very large, a simple curved stone that had engraved on it the crest of each town that had been attacked during the Cornwall massacre. Below each crest were the names of the people who had died in each of the towns. As Stuart and Jane stood side by side and once again read the long lists, tears gathered in their eyes and then fell freely down their cheeks. Jane said, "So many innocent people dead; it just breaks my heart. So many families and communities shattered and scared..."

Stuart responded, "They will never be forgotten. I have issued a standing order that every member of the Angels, regardless of rank, myself included, will be required to come up here at least once every six months and be part of the cleaning detail. That means that on a rota system this memorial will be cleaned every day of the year. As the men and women clean the memorial, they will read the names and remember the tragedy. And they will also be reminded of why this unit came into being; we exist to ensure that this will never again happen in the UK."

Hand in hand they moved on to the next memorial; this one was smaller and shaped like the unit's badge, the Osprey. Set into the black granite was a silver cross, bearing the name of Corporal Chris Cook, MC. Chris had been the unit's only fatality so far, the low casualty rate a testimony to God's keeping hand.

Stuart reached out his hand to the cold stone; the tears were falling freely now. "He was a good man," he said, his voice thick with grief and emotion. Jane reached out and took her husband's hand again. Only she really understood the depth of Stuart's feeling for each one of those under his care. He took them deeply into his heart, and the loss of one grieved him deeply.

They turned and walked back along the cliff, coming to a standstill where they had begun. Jane turned and gathered her husband close and said, "We have so much to be thankful for. Trish and Lauren are out of hospital. Bugs seems to have fallen for Lauren, but she is enjoying the chase. We have two wonderful children and their spouses. Two incredible, though noisy, grandchildren and another two on the way. And...," she said with a twinkle in her eye, "I no longer have a portly husband; he has been replaced with this really slim, dapper gentleman... who can be a bit grumpy at times."

Stuart laughed and said, "Amen to that!"

Their eyes locked then, and their lips met in a deep kiss of shared passion, friendship and respect. They both felt the deep satisfaction and peace of a life lived on God's terms. What would the next chapter of this amazing journey hold?

~~~~~
~~~~~

Hidden deep within the hold of a rusty, old freighter, Omar and Hussain began the dangerous journey to Syria and then Iran. Omar's mind and heart were full of hate for the 'kuffar', the infidels. He knew one day he would return.

As he drifted off to sleep, visions of a Caliph ruling a Caliphate under a black flag drifted across his mind...

The End

GLOSSARY

Call sign: a unique name to identify an individual group of men in the armed forces

Contact: an engagement between two opposing forces

Copy you fives: A term used to confirm you are receiving the radio signal strongly; one is the weakest signal, five is the strongest

Gillie suit: a coverall suit that is camouflaged and covered with different foliage to break up the human form

Go-bag: a bag full of the Special Force soldier's kit that is kept ready at all times so that they can deploy at a moment's notice

Hon: honey; an affectionate term for a loved one

Intel: intelligence that is collected to give the most up-to-date information and insights

IT: Information Technology

Mags: the magazine for a rifle; it holds the bullets or rounds for the rifle

MMTC: Main Man That Counts, usually the leader of a group

NVGs: Night Vision Goggles

Operators: the term used to describe Special Force soldiers, used by many Special Force units worldwide

RIB: Rigid Inflatable Boat

Shemagh: chequered head scarf used in Middle Eastern countries, but also by many special force groups worldwide

Stat: immediately

Stop-group: a group of soldiers positioned in key areas to block the flight of the enemy

Terrs: terrorists